Bolton
Council

Please return/ renew this item
by the last date shown.
Books may also be renewed by
phone or the Internet.
Tel: 01204 332384
www.bolton.gov.uk/libraries

BR

JF

THE DUNDOODLE MYSTERIES

THE DENTIST OF DARKNESS

DAVID O'CONNELL

ILLUSTRATED BY
CLAIRE POWELL

BLOOMSBURY
CHILDREN'S BOOKS

LONDON OXFORD NEW YORK NEW DELHI SYDNEY

BLOOMSBURY CHILDREN'S BOOKS
Bloomsbury Publishing Plc
50 Bedford Square, London WC1B 3DP, UK

BLOOMSBURY, BLOOMSBURY CHILDREN'S BOOKS and the
Diana logo are trademarks of Bloomsbury Publishing Plc

First published in Great Britain in 2019 by Bloomsbury Publishing Plc

A catalogue record for this book is available from the British Library

ISBN: PB: 978-1-4088-8708-0; eBook: 978-1-4088-8707-3

2 4 6 8 10 9 7 5 3 1

Typeset by RefineCatch Limited, Bungay, Suffolk

Printed and bound in Great Britain by CPI Group (UK) Ltd,
Croydon CR0 4YY

To find out more about our authors and books visit www.bloomsbury.com
and sign up for our newsletters

For Mum

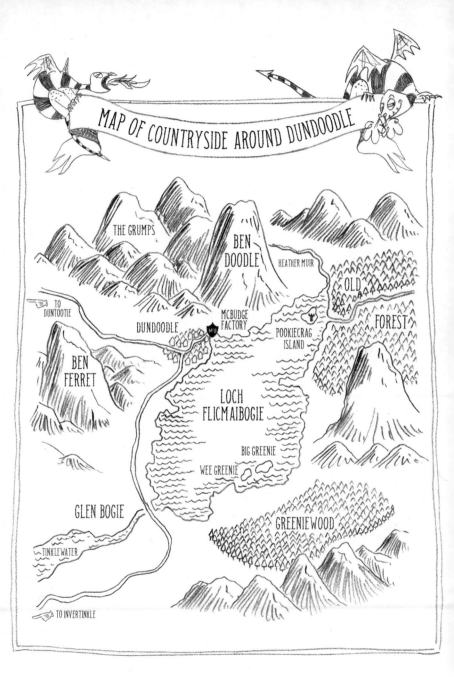

The hills were alive with the sound of … *dragons*.

Archie McBudge lay back on the sun-warmed grass and watched as a flock of honey dragons circled overhead, their little wings a blur of skin and scales. Occasionally, jets of fire would erupt from their mouths, leaving clouds of sunset-coloured smoke trailing across the blue of the summer sky.

'Completely bonkers!' sighed Fliss. She stood on a rock nearby, one that overlooked the blanket of heather and gave a view across the hidden valley all the way down to the loch. 'If anyone had told me last year that I'd be friends with dragons, I'd have said they were completely *bonkers*!'

Archie grinned and grabbed a piece of McBudge Fudge from his bag and popped it into his mouth. His friend

Fliss loved watching the honey dragons. He had to admit he couldn't think of a better way to spend a Saturday morning.

The two children looked on as the small, amiable creatures descended and then buzzed about the heather, making a noise like the hum of a thousand bees. Archie's little dog Sherbet barked and wagged his tail every time a dragon swooped close by them. He wanted to play chase but the dragons' wings gave them an unfair advantage.

'Careful, Sherbet,' Archie warned. 'You'll be a dog kebab if you get too close.' Dragons from old stories and legends used their fiery breath to barbecue courageous, armoured knights like they were human-shaped baked potatoes wrapped in tin foil. Not the honey dragons. They were more like flying blowtorches, but they could still do some damage.

One dragon paused briefly nearby. Its long, thin tongue whipped out of its golden mouth and deftly licked the nectar from each tiny flower in a row.

'Do they eat all the nectar?' Archie said, sitting up on his elbows. 'Don't they need it to make honeystone?' Fliss had become something of an expert on honey dragons, ever since one – named Blossom – had hitched a ride home in her pocket. Archie would never forget that snowy winter's night when they had first discovered the honey dragons, in the Cavern of Honeystone.

'They have cheek pouches,' she explained. 'They're like flying-lizard-bee-hamsters! They store some nectar in their pouches and use their magical Dragon-fire to spit it out as crystals of honeystone when they get back to the cavern.' She screwed up her nose. 'Honeystone is magical dragon drool. It's a bit gross, if you think about it too hard.'

Archie wrinkled his nose, remembering the massive cave filled with honeystone, hidden under the mountain of Ben Doodle. He, Fliss and their friend Billy had discovered it whilst on a quest to prove Archie was worthy of inheriting the world-famous McBudge Chocolate Factory and all the magic that came with it. They had never imagined the sparkling honeystone was made of dragon spit.

'We'd better get back home,' Archie said, getting to his feet. 'Or Billy will think we've abandoned him in the library.'

'Don't worry – you know he's in his element. Billy loves your great-uncle Archibald's collection of books. It's all material for his *Book of Wyrdiness*.' Billy Macabre (whose real name was Billy MacCrabbie) was obsessed with collecting stories about local legends and magical mysteries – or *wyrdiness* as the people of Dundoodle called it.

'I'm more worried about him stumbling across another secret passage or a hidden trapdoor into a dungeon. There are still so many rooms in that house I've not explored. We might never find him again!' Archie grinned at the idea. 'And anyway,' he added, 'I'm supposed to be going to the dentist before lunch.'

Fliss jumped down from the rock and whistled. One of the honey dragons sped over and landed lightly on her shoulder.

'You've got Blossom well trained,' laughed Archie. 'I wish Sherbet was that obedient.'

'The honey dragons are really intelligent,' said Fliss. 'I'm teaching Blossom to speak human. Isn't that right, Blossom?'

'Completely bonkers!' croaked Blossom in reply, burping a smoke ring into Fliss's face.

They left the other dragons to their nectar-gathering in the heather and tramped across the moor, following a sheep track down to the shore of the loch. As they trudged along the path that would lead them back to the little town of Dundoodle, Archie suddenly had the feeling they were being watched. A movement in the bracken caught his eye and he froze as a small figure appeared in front of them.

Sherbet growled at the stranger, a bearded man with a mud-splashed face. He wore a green hood and a cloak made of leaves. Clumps of grass sprouted from his moss-coloured trousers. The odd character bowed low, disturbing a little robin that was nestled in his beard.

'Guardian,' the man said solemnly. He had a strange accent. 'You are summoned. The Tree sends its first signal. A time of great danger is upon us!' He produced a large, yellow leaf from under his cloak and handed it to Archie. The man eyed Archie's face expectantly.

'Um ... thanks?' said Archie. The stranger gave him a confused frown before plunging back into the undergrowth.

'Wait!' called Archie, but the small man had disappeared.

'Who was that walking compost-heap?' said Fliss. 'What was he talking about?'

'The Tree,' said Archie, staring at the golden leaf that lay on the palm of his hand. 'This is from the Wyrdie Tree ... the source of all magic in Dundoodle!'

2

They hurried back to Dundoodle as fast as they could.

As they walked, Archie gazed across the loch to the dark and menacing forest on the far side. Somewhere in there was the Wyrdie Tree, whose roots stretched far underneath the strange little town, spreading the Tree's magic with them. Archie knew that the McBudge family were Guardians of the Tree, bound to protect the magic of Dundoodle, but he had yet to even set foot in the forest.

Finally, they reached the gates of Honeystone Hall, the grand, ancient and dust-filled home of the McBudges. Blossom flitted away to the giant greenhouse at the back of the building, where she had made her home amongst the tropical plants housed there. Meanwhile, Sherbet had dashed up the drive and into the hallway, and was sniffing at the doors of the library. They found Billy inside, sat at the carved oak desk and surrounded by piles of old books, scrolls and other papers. He looked up at his friends as they entered the room, his big eyes even more extra-wide than normal.

'You look like you've seen a ghost,' said Archie, glancing up at the portrait of Great-Uncle Archibald. The painting had been haunted by the ghost of his great-uncle when Archie first arrived at the Hall. The face in the picture hadn't moved or talked in a while now, and Archie wondered if he'd ever see the old phantom again.

'Better than that!' said Billy. 'I never realised this library was such a treasure chest of wyrdiology! I've discovered so many new things.' He pointed at a page in

a fat, red book Archie recognised as the *Encyclopaedia Dundoodilicus*. 'Did you know there's a were-squirrel that haunts the woods near Duntootie? Its fangs can reduce a spruce tree to toothpicks in less than a minute. Five point two on the Macabre Creepy Scale!'

'Never mind about that!' said Fliss, slamming the encyclopaedia shut so that a small cloud of dust blew into his surprised face. 'Archie has had a summons. From the Wyrdie Tree.' She told Billy about their meeting with the odd little man.

'I wish I'd been there,' groaned Billy as he examined the leaf reverently. 'You're such a wyrdie-magnet, Archie.'

'Remember what your great-uncle's ghost said, Archie?' Fliss continued. 'That you'll develop magical powers ...?'

'*Wyrdworking*,' interrupted Billy. 'That's what it's called.'

'Well this is your chance to find out all about it at the source!' Fliss said, giving Billy an annoyed prod with her elbow. 'You've *got* to go and find the Wyrdie Tree, haven't you? And we'll come along too, naturally. It's not every day you get to see paranormal plant-life.'

Archie flopped down on to the big leather sofa that sat in front of the fireplace and sighed.

'I'm not sure I'm ready for another adventure,' he said. 'Me and Mum haven't been living in Dundoodle very long, and what with looking after the chocolate factory *and* Honeystone Hall we've got quite enough on our plate already. I'm not ready for magical powers. I just want a normal life for a bit.'

'But this is *big*,' pleaded Billy. 'Like, the ultimate in bigness. It would be the icing on the cake of my career of investigating wyrdiness. So far I've only got a few stale, crumbly bits and burnt raisins.'

'And besides,' said Fliss, 'Leafy McMudface, or whoever it was, talked about a "great danger". McBudges don't have normal lives. They have *destinies*. And there's no running away from yours.'

At that moment, normality arrived in the shape of Archie's mum. Archie put his finger to his lips. If Mum had known about the children's magical adventures, she'd have gone, as Fliss often put it, completely bonkers.

'Archie,' Mum called from the hallway. 'We need to go, it's time for your visit to the dentist. I'll give you a lift on my way to my meeting with one of our suppliers. But hurry, I'm late as it is.'

'Is that normal enough for you?' said Fliss, grinning. She grabbed Billy by the arm and dragged him out of the library. 'We'll see you later!'

'What was Fliss talking about in there?' said Mum, as

she and Archie got into the car. She was using her 'worried mum' voice. 'About McBudges not having "normal lives"? You've settled in Dundoodle quite nicely, haven't you?'

'Yes – I have!' Archie reassured her. He had some celebrity in the town, as the new owner of the chocolate factory and the business that went with it, and that had led to some teasing at his new school. But he had plenty of friends and the teasing was nothing compared to what he had faced from the Puddingham-Pye family: Cousin Jacqui and her foul children, the twins Georgie and Portia. Mrs Puddingham-Pye wanted Archie's magical inheritance for herself and was quite happy to employ her children to try and bump him off so she could get it. Apart from that, Archie loved his new home. 'I still haven't got my head around everything,' he said, which was the truth.

Mum smiled sympathetically. A lot had happened in a short time, and it had only been a few years since Archie's dad had died. There was a thoughtful silence as they drove through Dundoodle's twisty streets. The town had a peculiar look, to match its odd character, with meandering, shadow-filled lanes lined by crooked houses. The townspeople had an air of the unusual about them too: there were plenty of eccentric folk around, oddly dressed or with strange pets or habits.

For example, they drove past old Mrs Kronkilty, who always wore a metal warrior-helmet with antlers – even in the bath, it was rumoured, using the antlers to hang her bath sponge on. Then they saw Morris Pimple from McGreasy's Burgers, who claimed to have a family of mini-yetis living in the café's deep freeze, amongst the chips. Billy said this was unlikely, as mini-yetis (Macabre Creepy Scale rating of four point three) were allergic to potatoes. Archie wondered how many Dundoodlers had *actual* magical powers like Mrs Puddingham-Pye. Or like himself, according to Great-Uncle Archibald, though he had yet to learn how to make his wyrdworking powers … well, *work*.

'Perhaps you need a project to focus your mind a bit,' said Mum. 'How about you talk to Mr Fairbairn about doing something in the factory? Maybe you could invent a new sweet or chocolate bar?' Mr Fairbairn was the McBudge factory manager, as well as Fliss's dad.

'I suppose so,' said Archie. He did want to do more to help the business and this could be a good opportunity to do that. *But do I have to do it right now?* he thought. *Why is everyone in such a hurry to make life complicated?*

'However, I want you to banish all thoughts of sugar from your mind for the moment,' said Mum, as the car drew up outside the Dundoodle Dental Surgery. 'I expect a clean bill of health from the dentist. I'd better be on my way – see you later!'

Archie grinned and jumped out of the car. Mum gave a wave as she drove off. It was as he waved back that Archie noticed the strange little man on the other side of the road, watching him from a dark alleyway, his camouflage cloak failing miserably in the grey of the town. The man scampered across the road towards him.

'The second signal, Guardian,' said the man, an earthworm tumbling out of his beard as he gave a deep bow. He handed Archie another leaf, this time coloured golden-orange, and just as before, looked at Archie as though waiting for him to say something. Archie was about to speak when there was a squeak of alarm from a red squirrel that had been hidden in the stranger's hood. The man let out a terrified cry and pointed skyward.

Archie turned to see a monkey-like creature swooping down from the rooftop, its leathery wings braking its descent. The stranger fled, disappearing into the shadows of the alley as the monster landed on the step in front of Archie. Its gargoyle-like face sniggered nastily.

'Surprise, surprise, smelly bratling!' the creature said. It was Garstigan the mobgoblin.

3

'What do you want?' said Archie, recovering himself. 'Haven't you got a handbag to go to?'

Garstigan looked fearsome – with his pointy teeth, bat-like wings and yellow eyes – but Archie knew the little monster wasn't a threat. It was his keeper, Mrs Puddingham-Pye, who was the real problem. Garstigan lived in her large, black handbag, and she sent him out to do her nefarious bidding.

The mobgoblin stuck out his tongue and blew a raspberry.

'The bratling should be pleased to see Garstigan,' he said. 'Garstigan has brought a treat for him.'

'Really?' said Archie, unconvinced. Garstigan looked offended.

'The roly-poly porklings are having a birthday party –' Archie couldn't help smiling at this unkind reference to the twins – 'and the bratling is invited. He is *most* honoured.'

Garstigan haughtily handed him a sugar-pink envelope with *Urchin* written on it (Mrs Puddingham-Pye could never remember Archie's name).

'There will be cake, and other yummy things that the porklings like to munch upon but make them fat and give them greasy spots and smelly, farty bottoms.' The creature giggled, then added daintily: 'Dress code is "smart casual".'

'It sounds *delightful*,' said Archie drily.

'There will also be *party gamesss*,' Garstigan added, hissing the words in the same tone he might use for *torture*.

Archie shuddered. Georgie and Portia's idea of party games would probably be 'Pass the Poison' or 'Pin the Tail on the Donkey', where Archie was the donkey and the pin was a very large knife.

'You must be joking!' he said. 'I suppose they want me to get them a present too?'

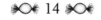

'Ooh, yes, yesss! Lots of pressies. With shiny paper and ribbons. Noisy toys and things that pop out and surprise you and make little bratlings chuckle. Like scorpionsss. Or dynamite. Or scorpionsss with dynamite.'

'No way am I going to this,' Archie said. 'I may as well be going to my own funeral!' He threw the invitation back at Garstigan. The Puddingham-Pyes must be up to something and he wasn't falling for it. *All I want is a normal life for a while*, he thought. *A bit of peace and quiet.*

The mobgoblin gurgled unhappily. Then it flapped its wings and kicked away from the step, hovering in front of Archie's face. 'The mistress will be displeased, bratling,' Garstigan spat. 'The mistress will be very, *very* displeased!' And with that he flew away into the sky, muttering miserably to himself.

Archie sighed and wearily pushed open the surgery door.

'You'll be seeing our new dentist, Mr McBudge,' said the receptionist when Archie gave her his name. He hadn't been waiting long when a tall, handsome man in a white surgical smock appeared in the doorway of the waiting room.

'Mr McBudge, is it?' said the man, flattening his black hair. His skin was so smooth it looked like it had been polished, and he flashed a smile so unnaturally white and even that it could have been chiselled from a block of soap. 'I'm Edward Preen. It will be my privilege to care for your canines, investigate your incisors and maintain your molars this afternoon, ha ha!' The man ushered Archie into his room and gestured towards the large chair at its centre. 'Have no fear, young sir, even though you find yourself in the enemy camp, as it were, ha ha!'

Archie smiled politely as he settled into the chair. He'd always looked after his teeth, even more so after he inherited the chocolate factory. There was no point having a constant supply of sweets if your teeth were too rotten to eat them. But he knew some dentists might take a dim view of the McBudge family business. Mr Preen loomed over him, his eyes staring over the top of his face mask.

'Open wide,' said the dentist. Archie felt the metal explorer tapping around his jaw. 'How strange that we should meet on my very first day in Dundoodle,' said Mr Preen as he worked. 'It must be fate.'

'*Awg?*' said Archie, screwing up his eyes under the dentist's lamp.

'Indeed. For it is in Dundoodle that I intend to launch my campaign, this very week.'

'*Awgaggawg?*'

'What campaign, you ask? A campaign to rid the world of the poison of sweets and chocolate and fudge, to drive out all that is unwholesome and unclean.'

'*Awgkeen?*' Mr Preen's eyes glowed steely-blue and Archie could sense there was a cold, perfect smile underneath the mask.

'Yes!' said the dentist. 'I believe it is my mission in life to make the world safe for children to grow up in. I want to make the world … *nice.*'

'*Aigh?*' Archie's head began to ache and he felt himself begin to panic. He realised he was trapped, at the mercy of this increasingly sinister man. He gripped the arms of the chair as the dentist scraped the metal tool along a tooth, like fingernails against a blackboard.

'N.I.C.E. Normal, Inoffensive, Cleansing and Educational. If it is not N.I.C.E, then it is naughty. Naughtiness will not be tolerated. And what is naughtier than a factory devoted to making sweets? Your business is very, *very* naughty. I have you in my sights, young Mr McBudge. Now rinse and spit, please.'

Archie furiously spat the pink mouthwash into a basin.

'I can't *make* people eat sweets, any more than you

can force them to *stop*,' he spluttered angrily. 'You have to let people have a choice!'

'We'll see about that,' said Edward Preen, calmly smoothing his hair back again as Archie walked quickly for the door. 'You'll be seeing more of me, Mr McBudge, ha ha.'

4

Archie had arranged to meet up for lunch with Fliss and Billy at Clootie Dumpling's after his visit to the dentist. The cosy café was hidden at the back of the McBudge Fudge Shop next to the factory, and its nooks and crannies were always filled with delicious smells. Miss Dumpling (who everyone thought might be a witch because of her sparkly eyes and her habit of knowing just what you wanted to eat) made hot chocolate that was famous throughout Dundoodle for its sweet, dark richness, and the children often used the café as a place to chat and relax after school.

'Why have the Puddingham-Pyes asked you to their birthday party?' said Fliss, after Archie told them about his encounter with Garstigan. 'I thought they hated you.'

'They don't have anyone else to invite,' said Billy. 'It's not like they have any friends.'

'Maybe they're trying to be nice,' said Archie. There was silence for a second before they all burst out laughing at the idea. 'Speaking of *nice* ...' Archie told them about Edward Preen and the dentist's threat against the McBudge Factory.

'He sounds like a total crackpot to me,' said Billy, dismissively slurping his hot chocolate. 'Who would want to give up sweets?'

'He's already started with his campaign,' Fliss said. She went over to the counter and picked up a piece of paper from a pile by the till. 'I saw these when I came in,' she said, showing the leaflet to Archie. Printed on it was a very flattering picture of Mr Preen's smiling face, beneath a banner with *Normal, Inoffensive, Cleansing and Educational* written on it in huge letters. Under the dentist's handsome chin were the words:

Stop the rot! Put an end to the unnatural pollutant of sweetness.
Join the N.I.C.E. campaign to promote dental and mental hygiene: clean your teeth and your mind!

BE N.I.C.E. AND BANISH NAUGHTINESS (COMING SOON: New, healthy treats for all the family.)

'Healthy treats?' scoffed Billy. 'They don't sound very *nice* at all.'

'Relax,' said Fliss. 'It sounds harmless enough to me.'

'I can't believe he had the cheek to leave these in here!' said Archie, screwing up the leaflet indignantly. 'I'll get Clootie to throw them in the bin.'

Just then, Clootie came to their table with a large plate of biscuits. She was very embarrassed when Archie showed her the leaflet.

'So sorry, Mr McBudge!' she said, flustered. 'He was such a charming man, I didn't realise he was up to no good. I don't know what I was thinking! I'll remove them at once.' She placed the plate on the table. 'Have a Gingerbread Dragon to make up for it – they're fresh from the oven.'

'Ooh, I'd forgotten it was that time of year,' said Fliss, grabbing one of the dragon-shaped biscuits.

'What time of year is it?' said Archie.

Billy and Fliss stared at him.

'You mean you don't know about …' said Billy.

'You mean you've never heard of …' began Fliss.

'Don't know about what?' said Archie, between mouthfuls of dragon. It was very tasty: rich and spicy with a soft but dense texture. 'Never heard of *what*?'

'*Unquiet Night*,' Billy and Fliss said together. A shiver ran down Archie's back at the words.

'What's that?'

'Unquiet Night is when the dead and undead walk, and the spirits and ghouls rise,' said Billy. 'Legends say the magical folk come out of hiding for the night and dance the Dance of the Wyrd.'

Archie frowned. 'That sounds like Halloween to me,' he said.

'It's *nothing* like Halloween!' said Billy hotly. 'What a ridiculous idea!'

'Dundoodle doesn't have Halloween,' explained Fliss. 'Halloween is at the end of October, and in Dundoodle that means icy wind and horizontal rain. The weather's so miserable even the undead stay in and watch TV! So we have Unquiet Night in the summer instead. It's always on the first Tuesday after school finishes – just over a week away. The town holds a festival for it, with special home-made food – spiced fruit punch, toffee apples ...'

'Coffin Cake!' said Billy.

'Witchberry Buns!' said Fliss.

'Spellcaster Sugarbeer!' laughed Billy.

'And Gingerbread Dragons,' said Fliss. 'People dress up in costumes and go around the town knocking on people's doors to get sweets.'

'You mean trick-or-treat?' said Archie.

'It's called the Wyrdie Walk here. Then there's music and dancing by lantern-light, all kinds of games, and a brilliant, creepy puppet show. It's loads of fun!'

Archie grinned. Trust Dundoodle to have its own special, spooky holiday!

'It's not *fun* at all,' said Billy huffily. 'It's a crucial time of study for a wyrdiologist. At least *one* of us is taking their responsibilities seriously.' He gave Archie a meaningful stare.

Archie sighed and told them about the second meeting with the strange little man, showing them the orange leaf he'd been given.

'I might be trying to ignore the Wyrdie Tree, but it's not ignoring me,' he said.

'What does it mean?' asked Fliss. 'What are these signals?'

'They are messages from the Tree itself,' said a voice with an accent Archie recognised. The little man was stood next to their table.

'It's you!' said Fliss. 'You were on the moor.'

'That was my brother,' said the man.

'And I saw you outside the dentist's,' said Archie.

'That was my *other* brother,' said the man, sounding a bit embarrassed. 'We've all been searching for you, Guardian. I have brought you this.'

From inside his cloak he produced a small, black, sleepy animal. Its velvety nose sniffed the air.

'That's a mole,' said Fliss.

'Sorry,' said the man, hurriedly putting the creature back in his cloak. 'That's Ingeborg. She likes to snooze in my pocket.'

He then presented Archie with a third leaf. This one was red.

'The final signal,' he explained. 'The Tree has summoned you, Guardian. And this time, you must heed its call.'

'I haven't had the chance, the other times,' said Archie. 'You keep disappearing.'

The man blinked in surprise. 'We thought you'd *know* what to do,' he said. 'But then we've never had a Guardian so young … You're supposed to reply, "the Guardian accepts the summons".'

'There's no manual for this job,' said Archie in frustration. 'What does the Tree want?'

'We cannot talk here,' said the man, lowering his voice. His eyes darted about the room. 'The Mirk could be hiding anywhere! Meet us at the Tree tomorrow. We will be waiting.'

'Hold on a minute!' said Archie. 'Why can't we talk here? What's the Mirk?' But the man had already slipped away into the crowd of customers and was gone, leaving only the smell of warm earth behind.

'It looks like we *are* going to visit the Wyrdie Tree, after all,' said Fliss smugly. 'We're having an adventure whether you like it or not, Archie McBudge.'

'There's only one problem with that,' said Archie, helping himself to another Gingerbread Dragon. 'We don't actually know where the Wyrdie Tree is ...'

'It's in the forest, silly!' said Fliss.

'But *where?*' said Archie. 'And how will we know which tree it is?'

'There has to be some clue to the Tree's location amongst all those books and papers in the Honeystone Hall library,' said Billy, as they left the café.

'Can't we just go to the forest and wander around for a bit?' said Fliss impatiently. 'Maybe there's a sign that says *Wyrdie Tree – this way.*'

Billy gave her a withering look.

'The forest is *vast,*' he said, stretching his arms out like a nerdy-looking scarecrow. 'And because the Wyrdie Tree is there it's full of enchantment. Even locals rarely go into the old forest. Paths are few and can lead you in never-ending circles. There are stories of people who have gone into the forest and have *never* been seen again. We could end up as food for wood waggles – Macabre Creepy Scale rating of six point seven – if we're not careful.'

They wandered through the warren of Dundoodle's streets, back to the Hall. Fliss and Billy were chatting all the way, but Archie was quiet. Even as they ambled up the drive to his home he couldn't shake off a feeling of unease. Not because he was getting involved in an adventure he hadn't asked for, nor because they had to visit the mysterious and magical forest. Ever since the stranger had mentioned *the Mirk*, Archie had felt a growing sense of dread. He wasn't sure why. He had no idea what the Mirk was. But now it felt as if he was carrying a great weight on his shoulders. The summer air was stifling and the afternoon shadows seemed to have deepened and become menacing. Today, the usually friendly-looking stone dragons that dotted the walls of the house appeared hostile and unwelcoming. He was glad to get inside, away from ... whatever-it-was.

WOOD WAGGLE

Mum phoned to say she wouldn't be home until dinner, as she had been asked to go to a meeting about the Unquiet Night Festival. The organisers were hoping to recruit her on to their committee. So the children went to find Tablet, Honeystone Hall's decrepit butler, to see if he could tell them anything about the odd little men. Blossom joined them, taking her usual place on Fliss's shoulder.

Tablet, who happened to be half-gnome and knew all about their adventures, was bad at pretty much everything to do with looking after a big house. In his opinion, dust was a form of interior decoration. 'And anyway, you don't notice it after a century or two,' he always said. However, he made up for it by being a brilliant cook – his famous walnut sponge cake was even envied by Clootie Dumpling – and they found him in the kitchen taking a delicious-smelling apple pie out of the oven.

When Archie told Tablet about the strangers and the different coloured leaves, a frown fell across the butler's already much wrinkled face. He put some meat scraps in a bowl for Sherbet and, with much wobbling, eased himself into a chair at the large kitchen table.

'Nothing like this has happened in all my time with the McBudges, Master Archie,' he said, as the children demolished the still warm apple pie. 'And I've been with the family a *very* long time.' He cackled wheezily. Fliss had guessed Tablet's age to be somewhere between ninety-nine and 'post-Jurassic'. 'But I do recall a story from several hundred years ago,' he continued, 'back when the family still lived at Pookiecrag Castle. Lady Archibelle McBudge, known to the family as Belle, received a summons from the Tree. That was probably the last time it happened. I don't know what it was about, but I *do* know it's too rare an event to be ignored.'

'I don't suppose you know where the Wyrdie Tree is?' Fliss asked the old butler.

'It's in the old forest,' said Tablet. 'Oh, you mean *directions?*' he added, in response to Fliss's masterclass in eye-rolling. 'Let's see, you go left at the first oak, then there's a patch of ferns, then … er … turn left again … or is it right?'

'We need to find a map,' Billy hissed at Archie, grabbing his wrist and forcing him to put his cup of hot chocolate down. 'Now.'

Archie sighed and reluctantly led the way to the library. Sherbet trotted along with them, yawning contentedly after his tasty meal. At the library door, Archie stopped, his fingers on the handle. A sweet scent had wafted over from across the hallway, and made him turn towards the portrait room.

LADY ARCHIBELLE McBUDGE
(1498–1560)

'I wonder if Belle McBudge is in there,' he said, remembering Tablet's story.

They peered into the neglected room. Cobweb-covered paintings of all Archie's McBudge ancestors hung there, their faces carrying the air of disapproval that old portraits always seem to have. Archie felt their disapproval was stronger than ever – did they understand his need to live in the ordinary world, just for a while, before taking on the responsibilities of being a McBudge?

'Found her!' said Fliss suddenly. In a corner – lost amongst other, grander portraits – hung a painting of a young woman wearing a jewelled dress and veil. The woman was looking into a gold mirror with a kind but sad face. Behind her on a table sat a little statue of a honey dragon, a common decoration in the Hall. The label underneath the picture read:

Lady Archibelle McBudge (1498–1560)

'If she received a summons, then it must have been about five hundred years ago,' said Archie. 'Tablet was right – the Tree doesn't send them out regularly.'

'She doesn't look very happy about it,' said Fliss, peering at the woman's face. 'Come on – back to the library!'

Papers and ancient manuscripts were still piled up on the library desk, where Billy had left them.

'There are *loads* of atlases here, bursting with maps,' said Billy, scanning the bookshelves. 'Where do we start?'

There was a rattling from one of the shelves above him. A pair of heavy-looking books were shaking and juddering. Something was trying to push past them, trying to get out of the bookcase from its hiding place behind the larger volumes. With a spurt of dust, the large tomes gave way and a small, tattered book hurtled off the shelf and slammed on to the desk, knocking a pile of scrolls to the floor.

'I think the library is helping us,' said Archie, as they stared at the book. It was leather-bound with gold edging. Archie carefully opened the cover. Inside, in graceful handwriting, was written the name *Belle*. A globe was printed underneath.

'It's an atlas!' said Fliss. 'Belle McBudge's atlas!'

Just then, a breeze blew down the chimney and swept out of the fireplace beneath the portrait of Great-Uncle Archibald. It gathered up the loose parchment and papers so that they flew and danced about the desk, a blizzard whipping around the children and flying into their faces. Sherbet ran for cover under an armchair. The pages of the atlas turned furiously, thumbed by an invisible hand.

'Wyrdie-weather alert!' cried Billy, and was about to give a Creepy Scale rating when he half-swallowed a dusty scroll that was battering him around the face.

Just as suddenly, the air became still. Paper and parchment floated lazily to the floor.

'What just happened?' said Fliss, dragging her hair out of her eyes.

'Look!' said Archie, pointing at the desk. 'The atlas. It's opened at *exactly* the right page ...'

In front of them lay a hand-drawn map of Dundoodle. It had been tucked inside the pages of the atlas. Archie held it up. He recognised the landmarks of Ben Doodle and Pookiecrag Island, at the edge of the loch. Dundoodle looked much smaller than the bustling town he knew. It must have only been a little village once. Dotted lines marked paths that led into the old forest.

'Where's the Wyrdie Tree?' said Fliss. 'It's not marked.'

'And which path goes to it?' said Archie, scratching his chin. 'These just wander around.'

'Perhaps it's a puzzle!' said Billy. 'Let's have a closer look.' He hastily threw a large book to one side to clear some space on the desk. A roar erupted from Blossom: the book had landed on the end of her tail! A ball of flame burst from the startled little dragon's mouth, missing the map by a hair's breadth.

'Poor Blossom!' said Fliss, scooping up the dragon into her arms. 'Don't be so careless, Billy!'

'She almost burned the map to ash!' the boy countered. 'A priceless, centuries-old document could have been lost forever!'

'Shut up, you two!' said Archie. The others looked at him in surprise. His eyes were shining and there was a smile on his face. Then he spoke softly to the honey dragon. 'Blossom, give us another fire-burst, please. Like you did just now.'

The dragon blinked at him in confusion, but breathed in deeply then released a gentle stream of fire. Archie held the map in front of the flames so that they lit it

up, but not close enough for the parchment to singe. Bright spots of orange appeared on its surface, forming a pattern.

'The light from the fire makes another pathway appear on the map,' he said. 'One that's normally invisible.' The others crowded around. A glowing, dotted line led right to the middle of the forest, where there was a symbol of a tree with a curling *W* written on it.

'It's Arcanolux Ink,' said Billy. 'I've heard of this – it's like invisible ink, except you need a magical light-source to see it. That lantern you found on the Quest would probably work too.'

'Now there's *nothing* to stop us from visiting the Tree,' said Fliss. 'This is so exciting! I can hardly wait until tomorrow.'

Before Archie could object, Billy and Fliss agreed they would set out from the Hall first thing after breakfast the next day. They weren't going to let him delay this adventure! He managed a smile, hoping to hide his lack of enthusiasm.

They had just let Blossom back into the greenhouse and returned to the hallway when Mum's car came roaring up the driveway.

'She looks annoyed,' chuckled Billy, as Archie's mum

got out of the car and angrily slammed the door behind her. 'We'll leave you to it! See you tomorrow!'

They grinned at Archie and scurried down the drive.

'How did your meeting go?' Archie ventured, as Mum stomped through the front doorway. She threw her bag on to the floor with so much ferocity that Sherbet scampered behind Archie's ankles for safety.

'It was all going fine,' she said, 'until some meddling misery-pants stood up and said the whole thing should be *banned*!'

'What?' asked Archie. 'Ban Unquiet Night? I shouldn't think that pleased many people. It's a Dundoodle tradition, apparently.'

'He said it was "unwholesome". What a load of nonsense! But some people in the meeting seemed to agree with him.'

'Unwholesome?' An alarm bell rang in Archie's mind. 'He wasn't called Edward Preen, by any chance?'

He told her all about the unpleasant dentist and his N.I.C.E. campaign against the factory.

'*Nice?*' Mum said bitterly. 'Edward Preen is anything but nice. I think he must be some kind of anti-fun robot in disguise! He even brought some biscuits that I swear tasted of dullness – I had to spit mine out into my handbag.'

Edward Preen was clearly going to be trouble and they would have to keep an eye on him. But Archie had other worries. After dinner, he tried to occupy himself with exploring the rooms off the south-west staircase, part of the house he had never visited before, but questions kept pushing their way into his thoughts. What exactly was he going to find at the Wyrdie Tree? What did the odd, little men want from him? So much was going on, just when all Archie wanted was a quiet life. The sense of dread had crept its way back inside him, chilling his bones and clouding his mood. He was beginning to feel unsafe, even inside the walls of Honeystone Hall.

Archie slept badly that night. He dreamed he was lost in a dense forest, the trees so close together he couldn't see the sky or tell whether it was day or night. Black, claw-like branches tugged at him, catching his sleeves and scratching at his face as he tried to fight his way out. A giant slug-like creature fell from a branch on to him, its slimy mouth slurping over his face.

He woke, with a start, to find it was only Sherbet licking his cheek to wake him. Archie drew back the curtains to a bright, sunny morning and the memories of his nightmare quickly melted away, though there was still a feeling of unease that stonily refused to disappear with them.

Archie had told Mum they were all going for a hike alongside the loch, which was only a slightly edited version of the truth. Tablet tucked sandwiches, apples and, of course, a box of McBudge Fudge into a bag, along with a bottle of water and some dog biscuits for Sherbet. Practical Fliss brought a torch and penknife, whilst Billy had his research notes and some Gingerbread Dragons. He was very cross that Edward Preen was calling for Unquiet Night to be banned.

'Whatever next?' he said, as they packed their rucksacks in the kitchen. 'Birthdays forbidden? Laughing against the law? Unquiet Night is *meant* to be unwholesome – that's the point of it.' He defiantly bit a Dragon's head off.

There was the sound of a car horn from the drive.

'Who's that?' asked Archie. 'I'm not expecting any visitors.'

The children left their rucksacks on the kitchen table and went to the hallway to investigate.

Archie opened the front door as a tall, pale woman unfolded from the driver's seat of a gleaming, silver limousine. She wore a white dress covered in an infestation of pink flowers. Large sunglasses hid her eyes but her red mouth was stretched into a sneer.

'Oh no,' groaned Archie. 'It's the Puddingham-Pyes!'

7

'Those villains always turn up when they're not wanted,'
Archie muttered. 'Which is *all the time*!'

Sherbet growled as the woman approached.

'Ah, Urchin,' said Jacqui Puddingham-Pye, silencing
the dog with a look. 'Dear boy. And I see your friends are
with you, as always. Fleas and Bilbo, isn't it? Stuck to you
like scruffy, little limpets.' She stalked towards them on
a pair of pink stiletto sandals. From the back seat of the
car, two blotchy faces leered out. It was the twins, Georgie
and Portia, plump and malevolent.

'What do you want?' said Archie impatiently. When
Mum wasn't around, he didn't feel the need to bother
with good manners towards the P-Ps.

'I only hoped to encourage you to change your mind

about the twins' birthday celebration. My messenger service isn't always as persuasive as I would like.' She rapped sharply on the black handbag that hung at her elbow, from which a muffled grumbling escaped.

'No chance,' said Archie. 'Why would you invite me? Unless you're planning to roast me over the birthday candles.'

'Dear boy. *Such* a sense of humour. We're merely trying to help you. Now that you're the Chief of the Clan McBudge, you need to be introduced to Dundoodle society. You need to be mixing with the *right* sort of people,' Mrs Puddingham-Pye cast a disdainful eye over Fliss and Billy, 'and anyone who is *anyone* will be at the party.'

'Sounds like a barrel of laughs,' murmured Fliss.

'You might not think it, Urchin,' said Mrs Puddingham-Pye, sliding back into the car, 'but you and I have common interests. Common needs. Common *enemies*.' She stared at Archie over the top of her sunglasses. 'We should learn to get along. See you at the party. Next Saturday at twelve o'clock. Sharp. I wouldn't want your mother to think you were being … *difficult*.' Archie hadn't thought of that. If Mum knew Archie wasn't going to the party, she would ask awkward questions. She thought the Puddingham-Pyes were rude, grasping and arrogant, but Cousin Jacqui and her children were still family and that counted for something.

The silver limo swung across the drive. As it roared away, the back window wound down and Portia stuck her head out.

'And don't forget a present!' she squawked, her face red with entitlement.

'Could someone explain what that was all about?' said Billy, as the limousine disappeared.

'She's definitely up to something,' said Fliss.

'It's just a question of *what*,' Archie agreed. He slammed the front door shut with a sigh.

'We'd better get going,' said Fliss, as they retrieved their rucksacks from the kitchen. 'It'll take us half the day just to walk around the edge of the loch to the forest.'

'Don't be daft,' said Archie, with a grin. 'We've got our own transport, remember?' He led them to the library and reached for a book on one of the shelves.

'Of course!' laughed Fliss. '*Ali Baba and the Forty Thieves*. How could I forget?'

Archie pulled at the book and,

with a *click*, the bookshelf swung away from the wall. Behind was the entrance to the secret passage that led down to the edge of the loch. The three children (and the dog) clambered through the hidden doorway and into the dark tunnel that lay beyond. Steps led down to a cave that opened out on to the water. Hanging from the wall of the cave was a silver lantern, its magical light constantly aflame. Archie took the lantern from its hook and, carefully wrapping it in his handkerchief, slipped it into his rucksack. Then he rang the summoning bell that hung near the entrance to the loch. After a few minutes, a driverless boat appeared at the mouth of the cave.

'Won't the boat take us to Pookiecrag Island, like last time?' said Billy, nervously stepping on board the magical craft.

'It knows where you want to go,' said Archie confidently. 'I've tried it out before.'

'You've been on adventures *without* us?' said Fliss furiously. She stamped on to the boat, causing it to rock violently and Billy to cling to its sides in horror. 'Archie McBudge, how *dare* you?'

'Only if you call going fishing with Tablet an adventure,' Archie laughed. 'His hands shake so much the fish have trouble catching the bait.'

Once they were all settled on board, the boat smoothly slipped away from the shore. It did indeed steer a course to the far side of the loch where the dark line of trees that marked the start of the old forest awaited them. On their way they passed close to the ruined towers of the castle of Pookiecrag Island, which hid the entrance to the tunnel that led to the honey dragons' cavern under the mountain of Ben Doodle.

'We should have brought Blossom with us,' said Fliss. 'She could have visited her friends.'

'Not likely,' muttered Billy. 'In the forest she's too much of a fire hazard.'

Eventually, they reached an inlet edged by clumps of silver-birch trees and gorse. The boat moored itself next to a large, flat rock and the children scrambled out on to the shore. Sherbet dived straight into the trees, stirred by the smells and sounds of the forest. Archie looked at the other two. There was excitement in their eyes.

'This is it!' he said. They pushed their way through the undergrowth and entered the enchanted forest.

8

A breeze – warm and pine-scented – swept through the trees and rustled a whispered welcome from the bracken. Wells of sunlight sank through the thick canopy of leaves, spreading a golden glow over the moss-carpeted ground, whilst floating pollen explored the morning air, twinkling in the dappled light like tiny, floating stars.

'This is definitely a place of magic,' said Archie, his skin tingling.

They soon found a path and, using the map illumin-ated by the magic lantern, carefully trod their way through the old forest. Tree roots carved up the earth beneath their feet or sometimes stretched out of the ground to make archways and tunnels. Sherbet ran ahead, occasionally diving into clumps of ferns to chase after squirrels (which were far too canny to be caught by a silly, clumsy dog).

'It's really quiet,' whispered Fliss. 'Eerily quiet.'

At that moment, there was a *crash* as Billy tripped over a root and landed in an undignified heap. A startled pheasant shot into the air, scolding the visitors.

'It *was* eerily quiet,' said Fliss icily. 'Do you need help putting one foot in front of the other, Billy?'

'It's all these tree roots – they must come from the Wyrdie Tree.' Billy picked himself up and dusted pine needles from his knees. 'I was trying to take notes as we walked. I want to document as much of this expedition as I can.'

'Just be careful!' said Archie sharply. He had the same feeling of being watched that he had sensed the day before. He didn't want to attract any more attention than was necessary.

After they had been walking a while, they noticed it was getting darker.

'The branches are making a roof over our heads,' said Fliss, pointing upwards.

'The trees are changing,' said Billy. 'It's certainly getting wyrdier!'

The trunks around them had grown into hunched,

hulking shapes, boughs twisted and knotted into sinewy limbs, twigs spreading into spindly fingers. The craggy bark was cracked into the features of ancient, wrathful faces, bearded with lichen.

'It's like we're surrounded by my grandpa and his bowling buddies,' said Billy. 'They look like that whenever they lose a game.'

'I wonder why they're so angry-looking?' said Fliss. 'Maybe they don't like visitors.'

Archie was reminded of his dream and shivered. The atmosphere had become oppressive, and the bracken tugged at his feet and made him stumble. He began to feel the dread grow inside him once more, only this time it was worse and getting stronger by the second. A thick mist seeped between the trees, turning their trunks into pale, misshapen ghosts.

Archie stopped, suddenly filled with fear. In the distance, he could make out a hunched silhouette stalking through the gloom. He grabbed Sherbet and hid behind a tree, gesturing to the others to do the same. The dog whimpered quietly. He seemed to know this was not the time for barking. They held their breath and watched as the dark figure crept closer. A buzzing, whirring sound followed it as it moved, as if it were being escorted by an

army of insects. Then the creature stopped.

It was cloaked. The hood slowly turned towards them, its hidden eyes searching. Archie ducked back behind the tree trunk, clutching Sherbet tightly.

Does it know I'm here? he thought, his head aching and sweat beading on his forehead. *Can it sense me, like I can sense it?*

The figure paused for several, horrible, silent seconds. Then, with a soft, stealthy movement, it continued on its way. It disappeared into the forest depths, and the strange insect-like sounds faded, along with the unnatural mist.

Fliss spoke first.

'What was … *that?*' she hissed. Billy was huddled on the ground, trembling.

'A doom wight!' he said. 'Or maybe a bracken beastie. Or a forest fungalfreak? Whatever it was, I think I might have to invent a new Macabre Creepy Scale – that was worse than … than *Auntie Doreen, with the moustache!*'

Archie was quiet, relieved that the feeling of dread – and his headache – were lifting. *Was that the Mirk?* he thought. Just its very presence had filled him with terror.

To one side, he spotted a clearing in the forest. A patch of blue sky was visible through the leafy roof.

'Let's stop there for a break,' he suggested. The others

readily followed him as he led them off the path. But when they reached the clearing, they found it was far from being a pleasant spot for a picnic. Ragged tree stumps scarred the area like yellowed teeth, and the trampled ground was thick with drifts of fresh sawdust. It was desolate and dead. Sherbet sniffed the floor and whined.

'Someone's been cutting down the trees!' said Fliss.

'No wonder this part of the forest looked so angry,' said Archie, running his hand over the sawn surface of a stump, as if stroking a wounded animal. 'It's been attacked!'

'Vandals!' said Billy. 'Do you think it was that scary person?'

'Maybe,' said Fliss thoughtfully. 'This was done with *man-made* tools.'

'Let's get moving,' Archie said in a hushed voice. Without another word, they returned to the path.

The map guided them deeper into the forest. The air cooled and became fresher as they travelled, the heavy atmosphere left behind with the scars of the clearing, and walking became much easier. The land began to rise, and suddenly the forest ended. They found themselves on a grassy mound. Immense, moss-mottled stones edged the rise, carved with pictures and strange letters. At the centre of the stone circle, crowning the top of the mound, stood a tree.

'Now that,' said Fliss, 'is very definitely a *tree*. With a capital T.'

'It's the Clan Chief of *all* the trees!' said Billy.

'This is it!' said Archie, swallowing hard. 'We've found it. It's the Wyrdie Tree.'

9

It was huge, towering over the rest of the forest. Archie thought he could see clouds grazing its uppermost heights. A mountain of yellow, gold and red, the Wyrdie Tree's canopy sprawled around a swirling mass of branches, some wide enough to support a house. *Are those windows twinkling amongst the leaves?* Archie could imagine an entire *city* of tree houses hidden up there.

As they walked into its dappled shadow, he could sense the weight of its magic, but this magic wasn't oppressive or full of dread. It wrapped around and comforted him, like a blanket on a cold day. He walked up to the massive trunk and pressed his hand against its bark. From deep within the wood, a rumble juddered through Archie's fingertips. Was the Tree welcoming him?

Billy dropped his rucksack on the grass and pulled out his black notebook. He began busily sketching the standing stones.

'There's so much to record for my book,' he said. 'I've got loads of questions. Is the stone circle some sort of celestial clock? Do the shadows cast by the stones tell you when to perform some important, ancient ritual?'

'Sort of,' said a voice from the branches above. A figure jumped down from the tree, landing on the grass in front of them. 'We use it for our washing-up rota.'

Two more figures appeared on either side of the first. It was the little men they had met the day before! They were dressed the same, in their green hoods and leaf-covered cloaks. One had the robin perched on his head, another the red squirrel on his shoulder, and the third carried Ingeborg the mole. It seemed to be the only way to tell them apart. Sherbet ran up to them, sniffing suspiciously.

'When you've been here as long as we have,' the first man said, as the robin gave Sherbet an aloof chirrup, 'it's easy to forget whose turn it is to do the dishes.'

'How long have you been here?' Archie asked. 'And *who* are you?'

'We came here with *her*, when she was but a sapling,'

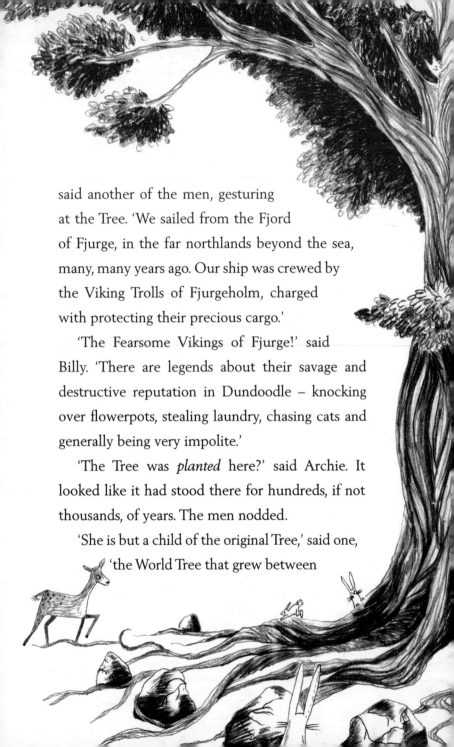

said another of the men, gesturing
at the Tree. 'We sailed from the Fjord
of Fjurge, in the far northlands beyond the sea,
many, many years ago. Our ship was crewed by
the Viking Trolls of Fjurgeholm, charged
with protecting their precious cargo.'

'The Fearsome Vikings of Fjurge!' said
Billy. 'There are legends about their savage and
destructive reputation in Dundoodle – knocking
over flowerpots, stealing laundry, chasing cats and
generally being very impolite.'

'The Tree was *planted* here?' said Archie. It
looked like it had stood there for hundreds, if not
thousands, of years. The men nodded.

'She is but a child of the original Tree,' said one,
'the World Tree that grew between

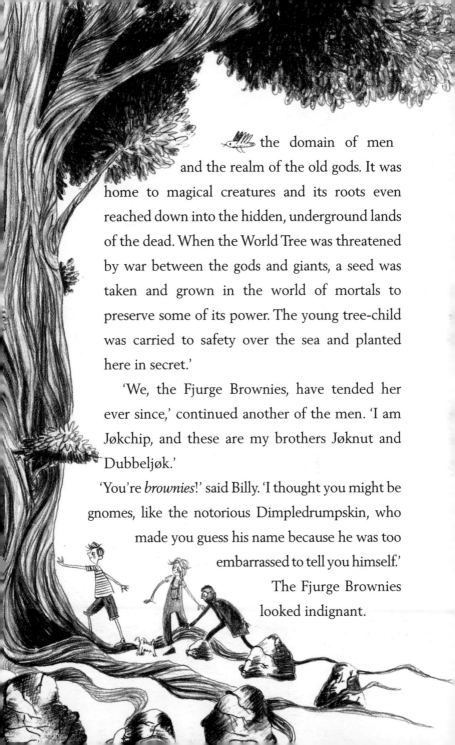 the domain of men and the realm of the old gods. It was home to magical creatures and its roots even reached down into the hidden, underground lands of the dead. When the World Tree was threatened by war between the gods and giants, a seed was taken and grown in the world of mortals to preserve some of its power. The young tree-child was carried to safety over the sea and planted here in secret.'

'We, the Fjurge Brownies, have tended her ever since,' continued another of the men. 'I am Jøkchip, and these are my brothers Jøknut and Dubbeljøk.'

'You're *brownies*!' said Billy. 'I thought you might be gnomes, like the notorious Dimpledrumpskin, who made you guess his name because he was too embarrassed to tell you himself.'

The Fjurge Brownies looked indignant.

'Gnomes, indeed!' snapped Jøknut, making the robin hop about fretfully. 'Useless creatures! Good for nothing but kitchens, or sitting on toadstools, fishing in ponds. Brownies are helpful household folk, but the Fjurge Brownies have specialised in gardening and horticulture.'

'Then why does the Wyrdie Tree need a Guardian?' said Fliss, looking at Archie. 'If you three are here with your spades and watering cans all the time.'

'The Guardian protects the *magic* of the Tree,' said Dubbeljøk. 'Your wyrdworking powers are needed, young McBudge. That's why she has summoned you. Her leaves are changing colour. Last week she was entirely green. It is a sign.'

'But I don't have any powers,' said Archie. 'At least, I don't think so. They haven't developed yet.'

The brownies looked at each other worriedly.

'That we should have a mere *boy*, at such a time,' muttered Jøknut to his brothers.

'What?' said Archie. 'What do you mean?' He didn't like being called a 'mere boy'. It sounded like the dismissive kind of thing Mrs Puddingham-Pye would say.

'It is the time of Renewal,' explained Jøkchip. 'The Wyrdie Tree only sheds her leaves every five hundred years. They change from green to gold, then to red, before falling on Unquiet Night.'

He put Ingeborg the mole down on the ground and walked up to the base of the Tree, to where the bark formed into a diamond-shaped notch.

'On that night the Guardian takes the Treeheart – the ancient Jewel of Renewal, a crystal fruit from the mother World Tree – and places it here. The Wyrdie Tree immediately sprouts new leaves, and with them comes a renewal of her powers. The wyrdie-folk celebrate with their Dance of the Wyrd, but during the time when her branches are bare, the Tree's power is reduced and she is vulnerable.'

'Vulnerable to what?' said Fliss. 'Magical greenfly?'

'Attack!' said Dubbeljøk, his eyebrows wrestling each other into a frown that was bushier than the tail of his pet squirrel. 'There are those who would harm the tree and take her magic for themselves.'

'Mrs Puddingham-Pye?' said Billy.

'Maybe,' said Archie. 'Or do you mean the Mirk?'

The brothers trembled.

'The Mirk is an ancient forest spirit of darkness,' said Jøknut. 'Its greatest desire is to control the Tree, turning her heart black, whilst stealing her power like a parasite. It has already tried once before – at the last Renewal.'

'When Archibelle McBudge was the Guardian!' said Archie. 'That was the last time the Tree sent out a summons.'

'And she was successful,' said Dubbeljøk. 'The Mirk had overpowered us, imprisoning us in a dark cloud of swarming flies. Using her wyrdworking knowledge, Belle was able to cast the evil spirit out of the forest. She saved the Wyrdie Tree! But we fear the Mirk has returned.'

'I think we might have seen it,' said Archie. 'On our way here, we hid from a horrible … thing. It looked like a person, but it wasn't. I could sense its power.'

'It must have taken some kind of human form!' said Dubbeljøk, turning pale. 'We suspected as much. But you say you could sense it? That means your wyrdworking powers *are* developing. You are sensitive to strong magic … but that means it can sense you, as well.

'And then we found the cut-down trees,' said Fliss sadly. 'Or at least, what was left of them.'

'We have heard rumours from the forest-folk – the dryads, the moss-goblins and the brook-babblers – of trees disappearing,' said Jøkchip, scratching his beard, which seemed to be made from moss as much as hair. 'Some of the missing trees are enchanted. The forest is like the Wyrdie Tree's family, the trees all gain strength from each other. Attacking the forest could be the Mirk's attempt to weaken the Tree further. It failed to take control of the Tree once before. This time, it will do everything it can to succeed.'

'Fear the Mirk!' said Jøknut. 'It is ravenous, relentless and filled with cunning. If it has hidden itself amongst man, it will be whispering its malice, and darkening hearts of those around you. It won't stop until it has what it wants. All things fear its hunger for power!'

'So we need this Treeheart-Jewel thing,' said Archie, frowning. 'Where is it?'

'We were hoping you could tell us,' said Jøkchip mournfully. 'The Jewel of Renewal is lost!'

10

'So essentially, the Wyrdie Tree needs to recharge,' said Fliss, as they trudged back through the forest, 'but we don't know where the charger is. Honestly! This sounds just like my dad and his phone.'

The Fjurge Brownies had been unable to help them further, so the three children had decided to head back to Dundoodle and start the search for the Treeheart there. Thankfully, there was no sign of the evil spirit on their return journey. Archie walked silently, absorbing all the information he'd seen and heard. Finally, he had come face-to-leaf with the Wyrdie Tree – only to discover it was in danger, and he didn't know how to protect it, even if the Treeheart was found. Why did this have to happen now? He felt useless, and afraid.

When they were safely back at Honeystone Hall, Fliss suggested they go to her hideout in the McBudge factory next door.

'We can use it as our incident room,' she said.

'Our *what*?' asked Archie.

'Like detectives have when they're investigating a crime. They put up a board with pictures of suspects, and lists of clues, and maps with bits of red string linking important places. If we use the library, your mum might find out what we're up to, and we don't want that.'

As it was a Sunday, the factory was closed, but Archie could still get inside, as there was a passage that connected it to the Hall. Fliss's hideout was hidden amongst the network of pipes up in the roof, a little chamber with walls of knotted metal accessible via a metal gangway.

In the eerie silence of the empty factory, Fliss took charge. She taped a large piece of paper to a broad pipe, and with a red pen she drew a line dividing the paper into halves.

'Thinking logically,' she said, tapping her chin with the pen as the others helped themselves to her sweet stash, 'there are two parts to the mystery. Let's deal with them one at a time. Firstly, the Treeheart.' She scribbled *Jewel-thing* in one section of the paper.

'I reckon the Jewel of Renewal was hidden away by Belle McBudge for safety,' Archie said. 'That's what I'd do. She didn't tell anyone where she'd put it because she knew there was no one she could trust, if the Mirk could hide itself amongst people, like the brownies said.'

'But she also knew the Treeheart would be needed again, as the Renewal happens every five hundred years,' Billy pointed out, chewing on a McBudge Marshmallow Cello from a packet of Musical Munchables. 'We've got some of Belle's books and papers – she must have left some clue for her descendants.' The boy's big eyes were twinkling. Archie imagined Billy couldn't wait to dive into a pile of old manuscripts and start researching. Fliss obviously agreed.

'Research is your area, Billy,' she said, 'so we'll leave that to you. Which leads us to the second part of the mystery.' She scrawled *The Mirk* in another section of the paper.

'We don't know much about the Mirk,' said Archie. He cuddled Sherbet as if he were cold, even though it was summer. 'We don't really know what it's capable of, or how to stop it.'

'Or who it is,' said Fliss thoughtfully, 'if it's taken human form, like the brownies said. The trees were cut down by tools, not magic. It's a lot for one person to do, even if they are magical – what if someone else is helping the Mirk, to weaken the forest?

'Who would want to help the Mirk?' said Archie.

'What about Mrs Puddingham-Pye?' said Billy. 'She'd like to get her hands on the Wyrdie Tree magic.'

Archie nodded, though it struck him as unlikely. Would Mrs Puddingham-Pye want to *harm* the Tree to gain its magic? He was reminded of the strange thing she had said earlier that day: *You and I have common interests. Common needs. Common enemies.* Did she know something already?

'Maybe I could find out more at the twins' party,' he said. 'I've a real reason to go now. I suppose I'd better get them a present.'

'Miss Clabbity's toyshop is the best place for that,' suggested Fliss. 'She does the puppet show on Unquiet Night … and Unquiet Night is only nine days away. If we don't stop the Mirk, it could be the last one she *ever* does.'

11

It was the last week of term before the summer holidays and there was a relaxed, almost lazy, feeling in the air amongst both the pupils and the teachers at Dundoodle School. The fact that Unquiet Night was not far away added to the convivial atmosphere. Gingerbread Dragons and Witchberry Buns were common breaktime snacks, and the children argued over how many sprite heads they would catch in 'Bite the head off a Water Sprite', which Archie discovered was what the Dundoodlers called the game of apple-bobbing. There was talk of what costumes everyone was making, and how many sweets they might collect on the Wyrdie Walk.

Archie found the mood infectious. Unquiet Night loomed nearer and nearer, without any progress in any of their investigations. It wasn't that Archie didn't *want* to do anything, he just couldn't seem to summon the energy. Every day he woke up determined to take the matter seriously, but immediately the sense of dread that he now associated with the Mirk fell like a weight upon his shoulders. The less he thought about the Wyrdie Tree, the less the feeling troubled him, and so he pushed the problem to the back of his mind. Billy and Fliss could only nag, and grind their teeth in frustration.

'Why me?' Archie said, for the hundredth time, as they sat in class that Friday afternoon, the last day of school.

'Because ... you're a *McBudge*!' said Fliss, who was getting a bit shrill in her exasperation. 'It's what you do!'

'Quieten down, Felicity Fairbairn!' called their teacher, Miss McTwang, who was a world champion in being shrill. 'Now, class, for the last half-hour of the day, we're going to have a lovely treat.' A murmur of cautious interest passed through the classroom: the children knew that teachers often had a very different idea of what made for a 'lovely treat' than they did. 'We have a local businessman coming to speak on an *important* topic.'

'Is it Archie McBudge, Miss?' said Ewan Fothergill, a spotty, sandy-haired boy, which got a laugh from the others, even from Archie himself.

'No,' said Miss McTwang, opening the classroom door. 'In fact, quite the opposite. Do come in, Mr Preen.'

To Archie's horror, the sinister dentist walked rigidly into the room, carrying a large, cardboard box. Archie had completely forgotten about him! Preen looked as polished as ever, smoothing his black hair down and flashing a cold, perfect smile at Miss McTwang, whose ears turned an alarming shade of pink.

'Good afternoon, everyone, ha ha!' said Mr Preen, surveying the rows of children like a shark sizing up a shoal of fish. 'What a fine example of today's youth I see before me.' His smile deepened the moment he spotted Archie. 'Some of you may already know me and know the cause for which I stand. I am here to talk about making the town of Dundoodle nice. That is, N.I.C.E., ha ha.'

Archie groaned. He didn't like the sound of this.

'No doubt you are all looking forward to your summer holiday,' continued Edward Preen. 'Such fun you shall have, ha ha … But I hear Dundoodle holds a festival soon, this *Unquiet Night*.' Mr Preen spoke the words as if they left a bad taste in his mouth. 'Girls and boys, I'm afraid Unquiet Night fills me with, well, *unquiet*, ha ha.

'A festival celebrating monsters and spooks. Silly,

foolish things. Things to frighten babies, ha ha. And *we* are not babies, are we?'

The class looked confused. No, they *weren't* babies …

'And dancing and music and other noisy foolishness. It's a silly, foolish festival. It is not N.I.C.E. at all. In fact, I think it is very *naughty*. And why do I think that? Tell me, what do you *eat* during this festival?'

'Skeleton Scones!' called Flora Twigg.

'Coffin Cakes!' said Nasim Hamdi.

'Gingerbread Dragons!' shouted out Ewan Fothergill, who let out a monstrous snarl. There were cheers and some laughter. Mr Preen visibly twitched.

NORMAL

INOFFENSIVE

CLEANSING

EDUCATIONAL

'Dreadful things. Not only superstitious nonsense, but full of fat and sugar, and ginger, a spice that elevates the body temperature most perilously. They do not belong in your young digestive systems, oh no. They belong in the *bin*, ha ha! What else?'

'Sweets?' said Heather McGumble uncertainly. No one was sure where this was going.

'Of course, sweeties. Little jewels of sugary poison, rotting your teeth away. Of no benefit to you whatsoever. Or at least, of no benefit to *you*, but lots of benefit to *others*. Others who make *money* from making and selling sweeties, ha ha.'

Everyone turned to look at Archie. Archie squirmed uncomfortably. There was doubt and suspicion in their eyes. Were they beginning to believe Edward Preen?

'Unquiet Night is about fun!' he blurted out, jumping up from his chair. 'And so are the sweets and the Gingerbread Dragons and all the other things that go on. You don't care about healthy things, you just want to spoil the fun for everyone!'

'Now, now, Archie,' said Miss McTwang. 'Sit down, please. I'm sure Mr Preen is thinking of the good of the community.'

'How true, dear lady,' smirked the dentist. 'Indeed,

young Mr McBudge is quite wrong, ha ha. For I have gone to the effort of creating a tasty, *healthy* snack to replace the teeth-rotting, sugary poison.' He opened the cardboard box, which was full of bright-white rectangular packages. 'I present to you the Preen Safer Wafer, a hygienic and cleansing chewy biscuit. It cleans your teeth whilst you eat! Each wrapper is even decorated with a little bow of dental floss. And I am giving one away to every pupil at Dundoodle School, for free. You see, I am not anti-fun, ha ha.'

'And I'm sure we're all very grateful,' purred Miss McTwang. 'Aren't we, children? I've already tried the Preen Safer Wafer and found it quite delicious! Now, it will soon be time to go home, so form a queue for your wafer. I have a bin ready for Gingerbread Dragons and any other sugary rubbish.'

There was some muttering, but the children went along with it. Some even seemed to be enthusiastic about Preen's Safer Wafer and said they had already tried it. Archie glowered at the dentist as he took his freebie, but the man just smiled triumphantly at him.

Outside the school gates, Archie was horrified to find Fliss and Billy about to tuck into the abominable Wafer.

'What are you doing?' he yelled.

'So you *do* care about something, Archie McBudge!' said Fliss. 'I was beginning to wonder.' She stuffed the biscuit into her mouth defiantly.

'It looks like cardboard,' said Archie, throwing his wafer straight into a rubbish bin. Fliss was deliberately trying to annoy him, and it was working.

'It's definitely chewy,' she said, trying to sound positive but making a face like she was eating a wasp sandwich. 'If a little bitter in taste.'

'It's worse than that,' said Billy in disgust, spitting out the wafer without even swallowing it. 'It's *wholesome*! To think, he wants us to eat these instead of sweets. What's next? Soap chocolate bars and toothpaste cookies? And

he's wrong about ginger being bad for you. It was used in olden days in medicine and potions and things – it says so in *The Book of Herb-lore* in Archie's library.'

'But I wonder if Preen has a point,' said Fliss, as she gulped the last bit of wafer down. 'About Unquiet Night just being a reason to sell sweets. People are always saying how Valentine's Day was invented by greetings-card makers and florists.'

'Don't tell me you're falling for his nonsense!' said Archie furiously.

'I'm just saying, you can't argue with his logic. Maybe Unquiet Night isn't good for us. And I've gone off Gingerbread Dragons, I must admit. Maybe I've eaten too many. This wafer could be a nice change.'

'Whose side are you on, Fliss?' Archie spluttered.

Before she could reply, Billy thrust the Safer Wafer's wrapper under their noses.

'At least we know whose side Edward Preen's on,' he said. 'Look what this says.'

Printed quite clearly on the back of the wrapper were the words:

Made by the Puddingham-Pye Cookie Company

12

Archie angrily crushed the wrapper into a ball.

'I should have known!' he raged. 'The Puddingham-Pyes are helping Preen to destroy the McBudge business. They'd love to see the chocolate factory close down!'

Billy nodded, reaching into his bag and taking a hearty bite of a Gingerbread Dragon that had escaped Miss McTwang's bin.

'It's pure spite,' he said, spraying biscuit crumbs everywhere. 'An act of revenge by Mrs P-P. She'll never forgive you for being the McBudge heir instead of her.' He passed a gingerbread to Archie.

'And *some* people seem to be falling for it,' Archie said, chewing slightly more carefully. 'Turning against Unquiet Night. I don't understand it.' Just as he'd found out about

Dundoodle's unique festival, everyone else seemed to want to ignore it.

'Oh, forget it,' said Fliss grumpily. Archie had obviously irritated her. He had a sudden urge to take action. It was almost as if the Gingerbread Dragon had energised him, reminding him of what he was meant to do.

'Come on,' he said. 'We're supposed to be going to the toyshop, remember? I still haven't got a present for the twins' party. It's tomorrow!'

They wandered into the muddle of streets and lanes, walking in silence. Archie was still bothered by what Fliss had said. *How can she think Preen is being reasonable?* he thought. *She's my friend! What hope have I got if my friends are against me?* But Fliss didn't seem to want to speak to him either. She trailed behind the two boys, dragging her feet, so that several times they had to stop and wait for her.

Eventually they found the shop: Clabbity's Clockwork Curiosities, Puppetry & Toys was hidden down an alley off the main street. Archie couldn't recall ever going past it before, but apparently old Miss Clabbity had lived in Dundoodle for all her long life. The shop certainly looked appropriately antique – its leaded front window was formed of little square panes of glass, through which the toys could be seen, lit by lamps that gave out a glow like candlelight. The shelves inside the shop were heavy with all sorts of intriguing objects. There were old-fashioned train sets and painted farm animals, and dolls of all kinds. Hanging above them, from their strings, were rows of colourfully dressed wooden puppets, their carved and jointed arms and legs dangling awkwardly. Around the window display marched a number of toy soldiers, which Archie supposed must be some of the clockwork curiosities. Their erratic movement was certainly curious. There was even a toy aeroplane buzzing in languid circles just below the ceiling. It looked very inviting, yet Archie thought there was something sad about the shop as they entered – it was strangely gloomy, and he could smell damp coming from its grey and dismal corners.

A bell rang as they opened the door, and a tiny round lady appeared from behind the counter. With her pile of curly white hair, unseasonal cardigan and tweed skirt she looked like she might have been knitted from a ball of lumpy wool. She beamed at them in welcome.

'Hello, hello, dears!' she said. 'And what can I help you with today?'

'I'm looking for a present,' said Archie. 'A birthday present for a brother and sister.'

'Do they have any particular interests or hobbies?' said Miss Clabbity, eyeing him over her spectacles.

Only death traps and assassination, thought Archie. 'They're very … creative,' he said, after a moment's reflection.

'A painting set, perhaps?' She looked around her shelves for something suitable.

'I like the puppets,' said Fliss, brightening up. 'You've so many of them!' She brushed her hand over them, stroking one that was obviously the grandma from Little Red Riding Hood and looked like a miniature version of the shopkeeper.

'Like rows of little corpses!' muttered Billy.

Puppets were obviously a subject close to Miss Clabbity's heart. Her eyes lit up.

'Oh, yes,' she said. 'Wood carving has been in our family for generations. I make them all myself. And I do the puppet show on Unquiet Night, you know.'

She went to the window and unhooked two of the puppets: a pretty woman in a long, velvet dress and a dragon with golden-painted scales.

'These are my favourites – the lady and the dragon.' She made the characters dance about the floor, her fingers gently tugging their strings to move their feet and arms.

'They're characters from a local legend,' she said, her eyes twinkling. 'I used them in my puppet show once – perhaps I will again. I do so love Unquiet Night.'

At least someone is on my side, thought Archie.

Billy was scribbling in his notebook. 'I've not heard that story,' he said, frowning. 'I collect local legends, you see.'

'Then you must have heard of *The Legend of the Coffin Creepers*,' said Miss Clabbity enthusiastically, 'and the lost tale of *The Mirkthorn*.'

'The Mirkthorn?' asked Archie. This reminder of the Mirk brought the dread back upon him so strongly he felt a little faint. He leaned against the counter for support, but fortunately no one seemed to notice.

'I've not heard of that story, either,' said Billy, fascinated.

The old lady nodded. 'It's mostly forgotten. The Gingerbread Dragons have something to do with it.' She put the puppets back in the window and took down another, a spidery tree carved from black wood. Its spiny branches were on strings, so that the puppeteer could make them writhe like thorn-covered tentacles. 'The Mirkthorn was a plant of immense magic that once spread its evil through the forest like a weed.'

'What's the connection with the dragons?' said Billy, watching the Mirkthorn puppet wave its brambly branches.

'I can't really remember. I don't think anyone is still around who knows the full story. You'd have to be very, very old – older even than me – to remember it.' Miss Clabbity laughed wistfully. 'Now I can only use this poor old thing as the forest that hides Sleeping Beauty's castle.'

As she put the Mirkthorn puppet back, Billy nudged Archie in the ribs.

'We have to get the rest of that story,' he whispered. 'It must have something to do with the Mirk.'

'How?' said Archie.

'How about straight from the dragon's mouth. We need to talk to Old Jings.'

13

Billy was right: Old Jings was the oldest honey dragon who lived in the Cavern of Honeystone. He must have been around the last time the Mirk appeared, and must know something of its history.

Archie quickly chose a Viking puppet as a present – he thought its large, ugly, wooden axe would appeal to the Puddingham-Piglets – and Miss Clabbity wrapped it in tissue paper, carefully placing it into a box for him. As she tied a ribbon around the box, a clockwork dragon waddled across the counter. Fliss laughed delightedly.

'How does it work?' she asked. Fliss loved machinery and had ambitions to be an engineer when she was older. The dragon even looked a little like Blossom.

'The mechanism is very intricate,' chuckled Miss Clabbity. 'It takes great skill to put a toy like that together.'

'Could you show me what's inside?' said Fliss. Archie and Billy could see the two of them might end up talking for ages.

'We've got things to do,' Billy said, impatient to go. It was mid-afternoon, and if they were going to see the dragons they would have to get a move on. 'Places to go. *Boats* to be getting into?'

Fliss was not taking the hint. 'I'll only be a minute,' she said dismissively. 'Why don't you wait outside?' She was still cross with Archie for snapping at her earlier, so now she was going to do things at her own pace.

Maybe we both needed a bit of time to cool down, thought Archie.

They left her with Miss Clabbity, discussing cogs and gears, and quietly stepped out into the alley.

'What am I going to do about Fliss?' Archie said, as he and Billy shared another Gingerbread Dragon. Billy was

still trying to get the taste of the Safer Wafer out of his mouth.

'Fliss is your friend,' said Billy, chewing heartily. 'She's on your side, you silly mugwomble – Macabre Creepy Scale rating of two point seven – but Fliss thinks logically. She's going to see sense in what Preen says, because there is *some* sense to it. That's why he's getting to everyone.'

'Once you dig a little deeper, though, you can see he's trying to manipulate people – the shiny-faced, tooth-twitching … !' Archie shook the puppet box in frustration, rattling the Viking around inside.

'Calm down! He does seem to be unnaturally persuasive. But you can't do without Fliss right now, so you need to make friends again as soon as possible.'

Archie knew he was right. Fortunately, when Fliss reappeared from the shop, she seemed to have forgotten all about their disagreement. In fact, she was in a very good mood.

'Miss Clabbity is going to teach me all about her clockwork machines,' she said, as they strolled back to the Hall. 'And soon I'll be able to make one of my own! She's so clever – she can build almost anything. Plus, she let me keep the clockwork dragon and she gave me *this*!'

Fliss held out a star-shaped wooden object in the palm of her hand.

'What is it?' asked Billy, studying the object's surface. Completely black, it was inlaid in silver with a zigzag pattern. He went to take it, but Fliss clutched the star protectively.

'I don't know. Miss Clabbity said it's a puzzle challenge for me to work out, to test my ingenuity.' She sniffed in Archie's direction. 'It'll keep me busy, as there's not much *else* to do at the moment.'

'Yes, there is,' retorted Archie. 'We're off to Pookiecrag Castle to see Old Jings.' Then he remembered Billy's advice. 'Look,' he said, more gently. 'I'm sorry I snapped. It feels like everyone is against me at the moment. I know I need to do more, it's just that I'm feeling the pressure a bit.'

Fliss smiled. 'Don't worry,' she said. 'If *I* was against you, you'd be running for the hills, Archie McBudge!' And Archie caught a cold look in her eyes that made him think she might just be right.

14

Pookiecrag Castle wasn't as haunted as the townsfolk of Dundoodle believed it to be, but the children were still grateful they wouldn't have to visit it in the dark. Its ruins loomed over them ominously as the magical boat carried them over the loch to the castle's island home. Fliss didn't seem to mind too much. She spent the journey focused on the star-shaped toy, trying to work out how to open it, whilst Archie stood at the prow, wondering if Jings would be able to help them. But Billy shivered in his seat miserably. He hugged Sherbet, who had joined them in the vessel along with the little honey dragon, Blossom.

'It's like the old bones of a giant,' he whispered in the dog's ear, looking up at the crumbled stone walls, as the boat drew alongside the castle's jetty. 'A corpse of a building, waiting to rise from the dead and terrify the life out of all the poor little sheds and bungalows in the neighbourhood.'

'It can't always have been creepy,' said Archie, nimbly jumping out. 'It was once a family home. Belle McBudge's home.'

'Do you think she might have left the Treeheart here?' said Fliss. 'Perhaps she gave it to the honey dragons for safe-keeping.'

'That's what I'm hoping,' replied Archie. 'Then we could get this business over with quickly.'

The entrance to the Cavern of Honeystone was hidden behind a trapdoor in the fireplace of the castle's great hall. It opened on to a long tunnel that led right into the heart of Ben Doodle mountain. There, in a cave filled with a forest of golden honeystone crystals, lived the dragons. The children arrived to find them busily making new crystals from the nectar they had collected earlier in the day. The cavern was filled with little blasts of fire and glassy, pinging sounds as the dragons spat out fresh honeystone on to the stone floor.

'It's a bit dangerous in here!' said Billy with a yelp, ducking as a newly formed molten crystal flew past his ear and ricocheted off the wall.

In the centre of the cavern, Old Jings was settling himself down in his nest. The biggest and oldest of the dragons, he was the only one who still knew how to use human speech. Blossom flew up to him, and squeaked a smoky '*Hello*'. Old Jings chuckled.

'Well, I never!' he said. 'Honey dragons learning the mortal tongue once more! You human folk are making quite an impression, for ones so young.' However, his scaly face lost its cheer when he heard why the children had come to see him. The dragon's golden eyes glistened with emotion at the news.

'So the Mirk is back!' he muttered. 'I've heard rumours of sightings. I hoped we might have seen the last of that foul being, after Belle McBudge dealt with it.'

'What happened?' asked Archie. 'Do you know what she did with the Treeheart afterwards?'

'I don't,' growled Old Jings. 'She would not speak of it, nor of what had occurred – it was too terrible. For on that cursed Unquiet Night, we lost one of our own. It was the last time a honey dragon died in violence, and the Mirk was responsible!'

As the dragon shook with rage, the children looked at each other in horror. What a horrible notion – the honey dragons were such friendly little creatures! What if something happened to Blossom? It didn't bear thinking about.

'We lived much more closely with humans then,' Old Jings continued. 'The McBudges were still in Pookiecrag Castle, so we saw them often. Belle had her own favourite dragon, just like you, girl. It went everywhere with her, but that was its downfall. All Belle could say was that it had spent its last fire defending her and the Wyrdie Tree. Her heart was broken.'

Archie thought of the dragon statue in Belle's portrait. It must have been a memorial to her lost friend. He could feel the dread and fear worming their way into his mind again.

'What *is* the Mirk?' asked Billy. 'Is there anything you know that might help us?

'It is an entity of darkness. A forest spirit. Once, it was a terrible tree whose branches spread like black tentacles, causing destruction and decay.'

'The Mirkthorn!' said Archie, remembering Miss Clabbity's story.

'The roots of the Mirkthorn tapped into the same earth magic that is the source of the power of the Wyrdie

Tree, but twisted it to evil purposes. The dragons destroyed the Mirkthorn tree, burning it with our magical breath. And that should have been the end of it. But somehow, through some dark enchantment, the tree's spirit survived. As a shapeless dark monster, it attacked the Wyrdie Tree to drain the forest magic for itself, but Belle defeated it.'

'We've seen it,' said Archie. 'The Mirk. In the forest. It was cloaked, but we could tell it was something to be afraid of.'

'It must have been in hiding for many years whilst it bided its time for another chance to strike at the Wyrdie Tree.'

'And we're still no closer to finding a way to stop it!' said Billy.

'Perhaps ...' said the dragon. It claws rummaged amongst the untidy stack of crystals that made up its nest, picking up and discarding various random objects it must have collected over the centuries – biscuit tins, broken toys, rusty tools, snow globes. Eventually, it produced an old book. 'The journal of Archibelle McBudge. Whilst she did not leave us the Treeheart, she entrusted us with this. It might be important in your search.'

Old Jings handed the book to Archie.

'Good luck, Guardian,' he called, as they left the cavern. 'The honey dragons will come to your aid, when the time comes.'

The sun was turning a hazy orange when they emerged from the tunnel into the long shadows of the castle. Blossom sat on Sherbet's back as the dog led them back through the ruins to the jetty.

'I'll get straight to work on reading the journal,' said Billy eagerly, as he clambered back into the boat. 'There must be some clues in there – there's no other reason Belle would have wanted the dragons to look after it.'

'We'll meet up again on Sunday – assuming I survive the party tomorrow,' said Archie. He looked around. 'Hang on, what happened to Fliss?'

She was nowhere to be seen. Then, after a moment, she emerged from the castle, looking a little dazed.

'Where were you?' asked Billy. 'Are you all right?'

'I ... tripped on a stone,' she said uncertainly. 'I'm fine.' She got into the boat and seemed to shake off her confusion. 'Let's get going,' she said firmly.

She looked her normal self, but Archie noticed she had the strange cold look in her eye he had seen earlier. And he didn't like it.

15

Midday (exactly) the following day found Archie outside the front door of Hardtack House, the extravagant home of the Puddingham-Pyes, which lurked on the edge of the town. Its straight, marble walls, bound together by strips of glass and steel, set it apart from the other, modest houses of Dundoodle, all porridge-grey and askew. In front, a precisely trimmed lawn was divided by a path guarded by two lines of conifers. A fountain, in the shape of a woman who looked like she had suffered an accident with a steam roller, spat water into a pond filled with glum, golden fish.

With the Viking puppet tucked under his arm, Archie nervously rang the doorbell. The door opened silently, and Mrs Puddingham-Pye arched over him. She wore a long, green satin dress with a high, round collar. She resembled a giant cobra about to strike.

'Urchin!' She smiled, venomously. 'So glad you could join us. Dearest Georgie and Portia will be delighted to have a little playmate. And I can't wait for you to meet our very *special* guest ...'

She stepped aside. There, in the hallway, as pale and welcome as a mug of cold, milky tea, stood Edward Preen.

'What's *he* doing here?' asked Archie furiously.

'Now, now, boy,' soothed Mrs Puddingham-Pye, placing green-taloned fingers on his shoulders and ushering him inside. 'Mr Preen is our good friend and a pillar of the community. And it's the twins' birthday – we mustn't let silly little things like *feelings* spoil their celebration. No one likes a crosspatch, do they?'

'Ha ha, indeed!' said Preen, his smile as cold and polished as ever. 'Feelings are such selfish habits. Not nice, not nice at all, ha ha.'

Before he could say anything, Archie was swept into a large, brightly lit room filled with people drinking from tall glasses with lots of ice and eating small but decorative bits of food. Polite, dull chatter feebly wafted about. There were no other children apart from him and the Piglets, who were sat miserably on a sofa at one side of the room. They had been scrubbed, and dressed in fancy clothes, but Archie noticed they looked slightly less round than the last time he'd seen them. Georgie scowled at him, and Portia screwed up her face so much her piggy nose almost disappeared inside it.

The twins' father, Tosh Puddingham-Pye, rolled over to Archie and shook his hand with greasy paws.

'Nice to see you, young fellow-me-lad,' he said. 'Look, poppets, it's Cousin Archibald.'

'Happy birthday,' muttered Archie.

'Is it?' snapped Portia, glaring at her father.

'Oh dear, if looks could kill,' chortled Mr Puddingham-Pye.

She's probably working on it, thought Archie.

'My little prince and princess aren't too happy on their special day. Maybe young Archibald has brought you a naughty little present?'

Archie reluctantly offered the box. He felt sorry for the puppet Viking. A grisly fate probably awaited it. Georgie immediately snatched the gift, jumped up from the sofa, and ran out of the room. Portia grabbed Archie's hand and followed her brother, dragging Archie behind.

'Come on!' she ordered.

'You little rascals have a lovely time playing together,'

beamed Mr Puddingham-Pye, in good humour. His wife watched silently as the children left.

'Where are we going?' protested Archie. Portia's grip was vice-like.

'Shut up!' she said. She opened a door in the hallway and dragged Archie through. Georgie slammed the door shut behind them. Archie looked around for escape routes. They were in a playroom piled high with all kinds of toys and games. Cuddly animals and dolls were scattered about, some with limbs wrenched off or with small axes or arrows buried in their heads. Archie shivered. They must have been target practice.

Georgie had just managed to tear off the wrapping paper from the present, before his sister tugged it out of his hands and ripped open the box. She pulled out the Viking, which rolled lifelessly on to the floor. Tears filled her eyes.

'I'm sorry you don't like it,' sighed Archie. He should have known the twins would be disappointed. They were spoiled rotten. They'd probably had loads of expensive gifts and all the latest gadgets.

'No,' sniffed Portia, her face all pink and puffy. 'I *love* it.' Archie was speechless. That wasn't what he expected at all.

'It's the only present we've had this year,' explained Georgie. 'Mummy and Daddy didn't get us anything.'

'Didn't you get presents from your friends?' asked Archie. He knew the Piglets went to a posh school in Invertinkle, so he didn't have to suffer their presence in lessons, at least.

'We don't have any friends, *obviously*,' said Georgie, as if Archie were an idiot.

'It's that horrible dentist!' growled Portia. 'He's the cause of this. He gave Daddy one of his wafer thingies and told Daddy that presents weren't *nice*, and Daddy believed him! And he stopped our sweet allowance. Preen told me that sugar and spice were *naughty*, so good little girls should be made of vegetables and vitamins instead.'

'It's like he's bewitching the whole town,' said Archie. 'Turning them against sweets and chocolate and fun.'

'Everyone except Mummy,' said Georgie, matter-of-factly. 'His mind-control spell doesn't work on her, so he used a Taciturnitas Hex on her instead. It stops her telling anyone what he's up to.'

'What do you mean?' said Archie, astounded. Although he'd used the word 'bewitching', it hadn't occurred to him that real magic was involved. 'A mind-control spell?'

'More like a potion,' said Georgie, giving him a sly look. 'I'm not telling you how it works – you're supposed to be a wyrdworker, you work it out! No wonder Mummy thinks you shouldn't be the Guardian.'

Preen has magical powers, thought Archie, resisting an urge to punch Georgie's piggy snout. *How else could he be having such a sudden effect?*

'We saw him put the hex on her at the biscuit factory,' continued Portia, cradling the Viking like it was a bearded, armoured baby. 'When he brought all the tree bark.'

'The *tree bark*?' said Archie.

'That's what they make all the Safer Wafers from. He said someone had a load of trees cut down, so he took the bark off them, as it was full of wholesome nutrition and the wafers would put it to good use.'

'That's why they taste like dead woodworm,' said Georgie. 'We refused to eat them.'

Could Preen be involved with the trees disappearing from the old forest? If that was the case, was he the Mirk, in disguise? The thing they had seen in the forest was human-looking. Archie's mind was spinning.

'But why is your mum going along with his plan?' he said. Portia smiled.

'She wants to know what he's up to, so she's keeping

him where she can keep a close eye on him,' she said. 'But once she finds out and stops him, then …'

Portia effortlessly pulled the Viking's head from its body with a gruesome *POP!* and flung it at the wall as a demonstration.

'That didn't last long,' remarked Georgie. 'I guess we'll have to keep playing with *you*, Gertrude.' He looked across the room to where an ugly doll in a pink dress and

bright yellow ringlets sat sulking. It was Garstigan! Archie hardly recognised him and almost choked in laughter.

'Not funny, bratling!' the mobgoblin snarled. 'Itchy, frilly clothes are not Garstigan's colour *at all*!'

Just then, Mr Puddingham-Pye poked his face around the door.

'It's birthday cake time!' he trilled.

'Cake?' said the twins together, their faces eager and hopeful. 'Actual birthday cake?'

'Of course, poppets! It wouldn't be a birthday without cake. And you're in for a treat: it's been specially created by Mr Preen ...'

16

Georgie and Portia's faces slumped with displeasure.

'We don't want it,' they said. There was a dangerous edge to their voices. Portia's hand moved towards what looked like a water pistol. Their father laughed pleasantly.

'Yes, you do!' he replied. 'Come on back to the party, poppets. You wouldn't want to upset Mr Preen and the others, would you?'

'Yes –' Georgie began, but it was no good. Tosh, using his considerable girth, shepherded the children out of the playroom, Portia hiding the water pistol in the folds of her skirt.

A huge, white cake stood on a trolley in the centre of the party. Ribbons of pink and blue icing decorated its many layers. Everyone stood expectantly around it, as

Mrs Puddingham-Pye stuck little pink and blue candles on to its surface.

'It doesn't actually look too bad,' said Archie. A shadow loomed over his shoulder.

'I take that as the *highest* compliment, ha ha,' whispered Preen in his ear. The man was just behind him, grinning wickedly.

Archie stepped away in alarm. 'I know what you are, and what you're up to,' he said, trying to sound braver than he felt. 'And I'll stop you.'

'Oh no, young man, ha ha. I don't think you *do* know, on either count. Also, I believe you are lacking a certain, shall we say, family heirloom? A *jewel* of some importance, ha ha!'

The Treeheart! He knows about it, thought Archie. Preen *must* be the Mirk! The dentist saw Archie's look of shock and his smile curled cruelly. Archie backed away, filled with terror. He was trapped, surrounded by strange faces in an unfriendly house. His head ached suddenly and sweat was forming on his brow, just like the first time they had seen the monster in the forest. *It's too powerful! I can't do anything to stop this!*

At that moment, Mrs Puddingham-Pye clapped her hands.

'Attention, everyone,' she said, gazing imperiously

around at her guests. 'It's time for birthday cake. And what a masterpiece of wholesomeness it is! Made from ground coconut fibre, grass seeds, grated turnip and other *delicious* ingredients, sandwiched together with Puddingham-Pye's patented Cremoliant synthetic cream and bedecked with toothpaste icing swirls. Completely, delightfully, sugar-free! Now, which of my two angels wants to light the candles?'

'Me,' said Portia. She stepped forward and pulled the water pistol from its hiding place and aimed it at the cake.

FWOOOOOOOOOOOSSSH! A blast of fire, not water, swept across the room, enveloping the cake and incinerating it in an instant, toothpaste swirls and all. Portia calmly turned off the device and smiled triumphantly at the foaming slag heap that had once been a cake.

'My birthday present to myself,' she said, blowing across the pistol's smoking muzzle. 'A flame-thrower of my own design. I call it the Deathbreath 3000.'

'She made that at after-school club,' said Mrs Puddingham-Pye, proudly, to the hushed, open-mouthed guests, as her husband gaped with embarrassment. 'She was top of her class in science this term, dear thing, and we *almost* got through the year without any teachers getting injured. We're so blessed.'

Archie wasn't listening – his fear had suddenly

vanished. And where was Edward Preen? As soon as Portia had unleashed the Deathbreath 3000, the man had disappeared. Then Archie saw him, standing – hiding? – behind a marble pillar, the crimson light of the dying flames reflecting from his perfect, smooth face. Perhaps the cake going *ka-blam* had upset him.

Whilst the guests warily inspected the cinders of coconut fibre and smouldering turnip, Archie decided this was a good time to make his escape. He tiptoed to the front door, but found the exit was guarded.

'Leaving already, Urchin?' Mrs Puddingham-Pye had got there first. 'We haven't even started the party games yet,' she said, raising an eyebrow.

'I've had a lovely time,' lied Archie. 'But I really must be going. I had a nice chat with the twins.' He gave her a meaningful look. The woman's eyes flashed.

'I hope you learned something ... *useful*,' she said. He knew she couldn't talk about Preen. All she said was: 'If you need me, boy, you know where I am.' She quietly opened the door and let him slip away.

Archie had never thought he'd find himself on the same side as the Puddingham-Pyes! He wouldn't ever be able to properly trust them, but it seemed, for now, there was a kind of truce in place.

17

At breakfast the next morning, Mum was in a bad mood. Oranges were mercilessly pulverised into juice, toast was buttered into submission, and tea was slurped with *extreme* prejudice.

'Anything ... the matter, madam?' enquired Tablet, arming himself with a spatula, just in case Mum decided to use the sausages as missiles.

Archie thought he already knew what the problem was.

'Is it Mr Preen again?' he asked.

Mum slammed her knife down on her plate, the sudden clatter sending Sherbet diving for cover under Archie's chair.

'That man is a *nightmare*!' she said. 'The committee to

organise the Unquiet Night Festival events is practically falling apart!'

'Why? We've only got a couple of days to go.'

'I'm beginning to think there won't be an Unquiet Night Festival *at all*,' said Mum. 'When Preen first showed up, a few people agreed with him. Now, half the committee have resigned because they think Unquiet Night is unwholesome. And, even worse, the N.I.C.E. campaign is threatening to protest outside the factory! I thought there'd be more resistance, but it feels like half of Dundoodle is sleepwalking its way around to Edward Preen's way of thinking.'

Preen's evil influence was spreading like a disease.

After breakfast, Billy and Fliss arrived. It was a rainy Sunday, but that didn't dampen their excitement. There was lots to talk about, so they hurried to the hideout. Billy and Fliss were flabbergasted when Archie told them what had happened at the party.

'You were lucky to get out of there alive!' said Billy, on hearing of Portia and her flamethrower. 'I wouldn't have wanted to be you, caught between the P-Ps and Preen and the cake apocalypse.'

'Preen is some kind of … evil spirit?' said Fliss. 'I can't believe it! He's a *dentist*. He gave Gordon McPlankton two fillings and a scale and polish. That's not exactly the kind of thing the Prince of Darkness would do.'

'That's why it's the perfect disguise,' argued Billy. 'He's respectable – whoever heard of a demon dentist?'

Archie nodded. It all made sense … or did it? A small doubt lurked annoyingly in his mind. Was it some wyrd-working instinct he had? He dismissed it.

'If we didn't already have a reason to avoid Preen,' he said, 'we've got one now. Keep away from him! We don't know what he might do.'

Meanwhile, Billy had been reading through Belle's journal.

'It's hard to understand some bits because of the old-fashioned way of writing,' he said. 'She talks a lot about her honey-dragon friend. She called him Corignis. She also mentions the Fjurge Brownies. I think she thought they were rather funny.'

'Does she say anything about the Mirk?' asked Fliss impatiently. 'Or about the Treeheart?'

'No. The entries stop a few days before Unquiet Night. There are just a few empty pages at the end.'

'Why did she give her journal to the dragons to keep?' said Archie. 'It doesn't make sense, if there's nothing useful in there, nothing to tell us what she did with the Treeheart.'

'Maybe she's still got it,' said Fliss. 'Maybe they buried it with her in the graveyard.'

'Belle McBudge is buried in Dundoodle?' asked Archie.

'Of *course* she is. In the McBudge family vault. All the McBudges are buried there, Archie. Maybe we should pay her a visit.'

Archie raised an eyebrow. 'Maybe we should…' he said. Billy's eyes almost popped out of his head.

'Are you *seriously* saying you want to go and dig up Great-Great-Great-Times-A-Hundred-Auntie Belle McBudge from her maggot-ridden grave and see if she's clutching the Treeheart in her cold, dead, skeletal hands?' he asked, in disbelief. 'That's *awesome*!'

'I'm not saying we should dig her up,' said Archie. 'At least, not *yet*. But hiding the Treeheart in a grave sounds plausible and, let's face it, we've not got much else right now.'

As they passed the factory entrance on their way to the church, the children were surprised to see a small crowd of people loitering by its gates – it was Sunday, and the factory was closed.

'They're N.I.C.E. protestors!' said Archie. 'Mum said Preen was threatening to do this.'

The protestors were handing out Preen's Safer Wafers to passers-by and carrying placards with slogans like

Sugar + Spice Is Not N.I.C.E.!
Chuck Out Chocolate and Stamp
Out Sweets!

and

McBudge Fudge is Sludge!

which Archie found particularly offensive, after all the trouble he had gone to finding its secret ingredient last winter.

'There are only a few of them,' said Billy lightly. 'It could be worse.' Archie gritted his teeth and kept his head down as they passed the huddle of people. He

had a feeling things were going to get a *lot* worse before they got better.

The three friends quickly made the journey across a rain-soaked town. Lurking in the shadow of the stunted spire of Saint Bawgbreath's Church, the graveyard was surrounded by a wall whose cold, white flints had a look of ancient, lumpy bones. Grass and wildflowers grew high around the graves and there were occasional cackling barks from a family of foxes hidden in the undergrowth. Billy, a regular visitor, led the way.

'This place is absolutely stuffed full of corpses,' he said with relish, guiding them on a path between the lichen-covered headstones, 'so no one new gets buried here any more. But the McBudge's still have a bit of space in their vault if you were thinking of planning ahead, Archie.'

Archie shivered.

'I am *not*,' he said firmly.

At the back of the yard, overhung by a large yew tree, stood the McBudge vault. It was like a miniature temple, all stone columns and depressed cherubs. The McBudge coat of arms was inscribed on its metal door.

'It's very small,' commented Fliss. 'How can all your ancestors fit in there?'

'This is just the entrance,' said Billy. 'The vault is *underground*.'

Archie pulled on the metal door handle. The lock was ancient and decayed, and crumbled away before his eyes. It took all three of them to open the door, its rusty edges scraping against the stone as it slowly swung open. Steps led down into darkness. The dead awaited them.

18

'It's not very inviting,' said Archie, feeling suddenly nervous. The ghosts of his ancestors might be hiding there, watching him, judging him. All the people in those portraits that hung on the walls of Honeystone Hall – they were *here*.

'Go on, it's raining again,' said Fliss, with a persuasive nudge. 'At least in there we'll be dry.'

She handed him a torch from her pocket. Archie wedged the door open with a stone, then lit their way down the steps. Billy kept so close behind him that Archie could hear his friend's nervous breathing. It wasn't very grand inside the vault. Cobwebs hung from every corner, almost as if Tablet had tried to make the place homely for its residents. Under the low ceiling, generations of

McBudges lay in coffins, stacked one on top of the other like tins on a supermarket shelf.

'It's quite crowded,' whispered Fliss, peering over their shoulders as they carefully trod their way deeper into the vault. Shadows danced around them. 'But I don't suppose they need room to move about. You could have a right old family reunion if you had a seance here, Archie.'

'Was that what you were planning?' said Billy, trying to keep his voice calm, his hand gripping Archie's shoulder a little too tightly for comfort. 'Only, I think I might go and get some fresh air.'

'There's no need,' said Archie, stopping. 'We've found her.'

They were standing next to a coffin carved from stone. Engraved on its side were the words

Archibelle McBudge
Departed this world in peace, 1560 A D

'Is the Treeheart inside?' squeaked Billy. 'Are you going to look?'

Archie hesitated. Belle had defeated the Mirk and saved the Wyrdie Tree, finding the Jewel of Renewal. She had done her job then and had earned her rest. Archie wasn't about to disturb her.

'No,' he said reluctantly. Then something under the cobwebs caught his eye. 'I don't think I need to.' A knot of spiders scrambled out of the way as he brushed the stone clean and shone Fliss's torch across its surface. There was an inscription on the coffin:

Seek the fire in the bite of a dragon
If by darkness you be pursued.
Look where my mournful gaze alights
One heart broken, one renewed.

'*Very* helpful,' said Fliss sarcastically. 'What on – or *under* – the earth does that mean?'

ARCHIBELLE McBUDGE
DEPARTED THIS WORLD IN PEACE
1560 AD

'I don't know,' admitted Archie. 'Why would you want to seek a dragon's bite? That would hurt a *lot*. I can't make sense of the rest.'

'*One heart broken, one renewed,*' read Billy. 'Maybe she's talking about the Tree*heart*, the Jewel of Renewal. Perhaps it's a spell?'

'We need to think about this,' said Archie, 'but not here. Let's get back to the Hall.'

He turned and stubbed his toe against something solid and heavy that was lying in the gloom nearby. It was a smallish wooden coffin. There were three of them, side by side, sat as if waiting for their occupants.

'They look new,' Billy said. 'Who are they for?'

Archie leaned over the first, curious to see the name that had been roughly scratched into the unvarnished lid. It said

WILLIAM MacCRABBIE

The next one read:

FELICITY FAIRBAIRN

Archie felt his blood run cold, as he looked at the third.

The coffins were for *them*.

'If this is what the g-g-grave-digger calls customer service, then I want to make a very s-s-s-strongly worded complaint!' stuttered Billy.

They ran back towards the entrance, stumbled up the stairs, expecting to see grey-washed daylight. But they were met by dark, rusty iron.

'The door to the vault is closed!' said Archie. 'We've been shut in!'

'Trapped!' squealed Billy. 'Buried alive, like the phantom Druid of Rubblehenge, Macabre Creepy Scale rating of seven point four!'

'I left the door wedged open!' said Archie, putting his weight against the cold metal. The door didn't budge. 'Fliss, you were last in – did you see anything?'

Fliss looked up at them from the shadows of the steps below. She was quite calm. There was that look in her eyes again. Was she even smiling?

'I didn't want to leave the door open,' she said coolly. 'It might have attracted attention.'

'Don't you see how dangerous that is?' shouted Archie,

as Billy joined him, vainly shoving against the entrance. 'What if the door won't open? It's obvious someone meant us to come here – maybe Preen! You saw the coffins, he could have been planning something horrible!'

'I'm sure someone will let us out. Eventually.'

'Fliss! Help us!'

There was a pause. Fliss seemed confused for a moment. Then she stomped up the steps.

'All right, don't get your toffees in a twist,' she said. 'If we all push together, perhaps it will move.'

They leaned against the door, their wet shoes slipping against the stone floor. With an unpleasant, metallic shriek, the door reluctantly gave way. Watery light flooded in.

'I don't think I've ever been so pleased to see rain,' sighed Billy.

Archie was silent. He was angry, and worried. Fliss had deliberately shut them in the vault. Was one of his own friends, one of the people he trusted most, actually his *enemy*?

19

Archie didn't sleep a wink that night. He knew the Mirk was dangerous, but it hadn't ever occurred to him that someone might want to harm him and his friends. And what about Fliss? She'd been acting so strangely. She wasn't her usual self at all, and he really needed his friends' help right now. Lying in the darkness, his mind clouded with fear.

Monday morning eventually dawned, sunny and warm. Archie awoke with a burning desire to stop the Mirk at all costs. Perhaps the Mirk had been using his fear against him? *Whispering its malice and darkening hearts*, the brownies had said. Was this what they had meant? He remembered how the dread had stopped him from taking action earlier.

'I'm sorry you've been dragged into this,' he said, when he and Sherbet met up with the others in the hideout. Blossom was with them sitting in her usual spot on Fliss's shoulder. 'Yesterday was pretty scary.'

'Forget it,' said Fliss dismissively, though she looked pale. She was playing absent-mindedly with the clockwork dragon she'd been gifted by Miss Clabbity. 'Someone's just trying to frighten us.'

'But how did they know we were going to the graveyard?' said Billy, who had been the most shaken. Sherbet was getting used to his anxious hugs.

'Preen must be keeping watch on us somehow,' said Archie. 'He must be behind this. It would be just his style of humour – creepy.' He picked up Fliss's red pen and started writing on the paper that was still stuck to the pipe. 'Let's recap what we know so far. We're missing something, I'm sure of it, and it might help us work out what.'

'Firstly, there's the weird rhyme in tomb,' said Fliss. 'Though that's not been much use.' She threw the dragon toy on the floor dejectedly.

'What happened to that black star puzzle thing you had?' said Billy, as Archie wrote out the lines of the poem. 'You've stopped playing with it.'

'I lost it somewhere,' said Fliss despondently. 'I can't think where. One minute I had it and then I didn't. I told Miss Clabbity, but she didn't seem to mind. I was worried because it looked really precious.'

Meanwhile, Archie wrote *Edward Preen* on the board.

'We know Preen's involved,' he said. 'I'm sure he might even be the Mirk in disguise. So far he seems intent on wrecking Unquiet Night and turning people against the factory, even roping the P-Ps into his plan. And he's been using tree bark to make the Safer Wafers. I'm willing to bet he got that from those cut-down trees we found.'

'If he's cutting down the trees, it will weaken the protective magic of the forest and the Wyrdie Tree, according to the brownies,' said Billy. 'It all helps the Mirk, either way.'

'To be fair, the wafers make a nice change,' said Fliss. 'Gingerbread Dragons can give you belly ache.'

'Only if you stuff yourself,' snapped Billy, 'and you won't be able to do that for much longer. People have stopped making them, thanks to Preen.'

'What?' said Archie.

'Clootie is the only person in town still baking them,' said Billy. 'I picked up one of the last bags from her shop on my way here, although it was a struggle to get past those protestors. We'll have to start making our own at this rate, which is the other thing I have to tell you …' He took the journal of Belle McBudge from his bag. He thumbed through the book until he found a page thicker than the others. It was a pocket, formed by two pages stuck together. 'There was something hidden in the journal, just like the map was hidden in the atlas.' He carefully eased a small, fragile piece of parchment from inside the hidden pocket. It was covered in words – a list of ingredients and instructions – written in Belle's familiar handwriting.

'A recipe?' said Archie, taking the parchment from Billy and studying it. 'A recipe for Gingerbread Dragons.'

'So what?' said Fliss. 'That just means she liked baking.'

'In my research,' said Billy, ignoring her, 'I've not found evidence of anyone making Gingerbread Dragons before Belle's time. I think this could be the very *first* recipe for a Gingerbread Dragon. Look, it's dated the day before the Unquiet Night when she defeated the Mirk.'

'Belle *invented* the Gingerbread Dragon!' grinned Archie, impressed. 'It *has* to mean something!'

'It's just a *biscuit*,' snorted Fliss.

'Then why is Preen so bothered by it?' retorted Archie. 'What could he have to fear from biscuits? Unless …'

'What?' said Billy.

'Unless they're magic,' said Archie slowly.

Fliss laughed. 'That's ridiculous,' she said.

Archie examined the Gingerbread Dragon recipe, looking for anything that might give him some kind of clue. There was nothing obvious. *But then Belle would have made* sure *there was nothing obvious*, he thought. An idea suddenly struck him. Belle's map that showed the way to the Wyrdie Tree – she had used Arcanolux Ink to draw the secret path! Maybe she had used the same trick twice.

'Blossom – give me a fire-burst please,' he said, holding up the recipe. The little dragon obliged, the golden light of her magical breath reflecting off the pipes of the hideout. There was a glow from the ancient paper. He'd been right! Under the list of ingredients, there were hidden instructions in shining letters:

Ginger is the most important ingredient, for it is the fire root that will keep the Mirk at bay. Then bake in an oven of DRAGON-FIRE *to enhance its power.*

Dragon-fire! The biscuits had been cooked by a dragon!

'The rhyme from the tomb!' gasped Archie, pointing

at the paper he had just written on. '*Seek the fire in the bite of a dragon, if by darkness you be pursued* – not a real dragon, a bite from a dragon *biscuit* with *fiery* spices!'

'You're right!' said Billy. 'The Gingerbread Dragons have magic powers! Powers that protect you from the Mirk! Preen must have known, so he tried to stop people making them.'

'Not only that,' said Archie, his mind churning, frantically trying to put pieces of badly fitting puzzles together. 'He made his own, evil version. Georgie said Preen was using a mind-control potion, but wouldn't tell me how. I've only just worked it out – he put it in the Safer Wafer. And everyone who ate one is under his control.'

'Everyone?' said Billy. 'But that means … that means …' He turned to look at Fliss.

'Yes,' said Archie. 'Fliss is working for Edward Preen.'

'Fliss is helping *the Mirk?*' said Billy, horrified. 'She – she can't be. It's not true is it, Fliss? I know you've been a bit cranky lately but ...' His voice dried up in his throat.

Fliss looked back at them with that cold look in her eyes that had so worried Archie.

'Think about it, Billy,' said Archie. 'You said so yourself, how did someone know we were going to the McBudge vault? It was Fliss's idea to go there in the first place – we were *meant* to go there. Then she shut us in with the coffins!'

'I can't believe she would do this to us!' said Billy, shaking.

'It's not her,' said Archie, grasping him by the shoulder. 'It's not *our* Fliss. She's being used, like the rest of Dundoodle. They're all bewitched.'

'Where's the Treeheart, Archie?' said Fliss, her voice mechanical and distant. 'I know you're hiding it somewhere. Where is it?'

Archie and Billy edged away. Sherbet growled.

'Where's the Treeheart?' Fliss repeated. 'Give me the Treeheart.' She reached out her hand to grab Archie's throat. Blossom, alarmed at the change in her friend's behaviour, let out a burst of flame. It swept dangerously close to the girl's fingers. Fliss screamed, instinctively withdrawing her hand from the heat. At that moment, Billy snatched a broken Gingerbread Dragon from the bag he had brought from Clootie's, hurling a piece of biscuit squarely into Fliss's open mouth.

'Careful!' said Archie. 'She could choke!'

'It's worth the risk,' said Billy. 'We have to save her!'

Fliss couldn't help but bite down on the gingerbread. As she did so her eyes warmed, and a spark of life appeared in them. She started chewing, slowly first then faster, the Fliss they recognised gradually returning. The spell was breaking! She looked around her, confused, as if she didn't remember where she was or how she'd got there.

'What's going on?' she said. 'I feel like I've been outside my body watching myself.'

She was furious when they told her what they had guessed about the wafers.

'It should have been Billy who was bewitched, not me,' she said. 'If anyone is pathetic enough to be mind-controlled, it's him.'

'That's really rude,' said Billy, 'but a fair point. Though I'd make a lousy henchman.' He didn't mind Fliss's insults, he was just glad to have her back to normal.

'I remembered how different I felt after I'd eaten a Gingerbread Dragon that day Preen came to school,' said Archie. 'Like I was suddenly shaking off my fear of the Mirk. That's the same time you began acting strangely, just after you'd eaten the Safer Wafer.'

'Cursed Confectionery,' said Billy. 'Macabre Creepy Scale rating of five point seven!'

'But who knows what else I've done?' said Fliss. 'My memory is really hazy. The Mirk could have made me do terrible things!'

'We can't worry about that now,' said Archie. 'Just keep away from the Safer Wafers. We'll have to ration the Dragons, too. There aren't many left.'

At that moment, a voice called up from the factory floor below.

'Archie, are you up there?' It was Mum. Fliss bundled Blossom into her bag and the children clambered out of the mess of pipework on to the gangway and saw Archie's mum looking up at them with a grim face.

'Archie, children – I've got some bad news,' she said. 'I'm afraid the festival isn't going ahead. Unquiet Night has been cancelled.'

They looked at each other, horrified. Mum explained as they hurried back to the Hall.

'The committee for organising the festival has resigned,' she said with a heavy sigh. 'No one is interested in doing anything, apart from complaining about sweets and talking about wholesomeness, as if they'd know what that is. Mean Preen has got to them somehow.'

'This is a disaster!' said Billy bitterly. 'Unquiet Night is the most important day of the year! This has *never* happened before. Dundoodle without Unquiet Night is like chips without curry sauce – *unthinkable.*'

'I'm sorry,' said Mum. 'It does sound like you'll be missing out on a lot of fun.'

'*Fun?*' said Billy, his eyes welling up. 'It's a day for *serious* study of supernatural and paranormal phenomena. Without the festival, the emotionally-generated psychokinetic energy field will be substantially suboptimal for *any* wyrdological events to manifest themselves.'

'Yes … that too,' said Mum, gently patting him on the back.

She left them in the library, each with a reassuring ice cream sundae with McBudge Fudge sauce, Tablet's summer alternative to hot chocolate.

'We need to work out what the rest of the rhyme means and find the Treeheart,' said Archie. 'We can do it, I know we can!' He was trying to sound positive, but the situation was urgent. Regardless of whether the festival took place or not, the Wyrdie Tree must renew itself. Its power would be at its weakest, and the Mirk was ready to attack. They got to work.

'*Look where my mournful gaze alights, one heart broken, one renewed,*' Archie recited, scratching his head. Billy was sat scouring Belle's journal, desperately searching the elegant handwriting for any clues he might have missed. Meanwhile, Fliss was looking through a pile of books on the history of the old forest, to see if she could find any mention of the Treeheart. She couldn't help yawning: it wasn't exactly riveting stuff. Blossom yawned in sympathy.

'You're not helping, Blossom,' Fliss said, smiling for the first time in a while. 'I wonder if Corignis helped Belle. Maybe he was the dragon that baked the first Gingerbread Dragons? I wonder why Belle didn't use a normal oven.'

Archie looked up from an old scroll he was reading, about the McBudge family jewels.

'Honeystone!' he said, his eyes lit up. 'Dragon-fire turns nectar from flowers into honeystone. Nectar's a type of sugar, isn't it? So perhaps dragon-fire turned the sugar in the biscuits into tiny little crystals of honeystone too!'

'So as well as making the gingerbread tastier,' added Billy, 'its magical properties might enhance the protect-ive effects of the ginger.'

In spite of the urgency of the situation, Archie grinned. 'I've had another idea,' he said.

There was no time to lose. Archie ran back to the factory, followed by the others and refusing to answer their questions. They found the manager's office. Mr Fairbairn looked a lot like Fliss and had the same logical mind.

'Hello, you lot,' he said, ushering them into the office with a welcoming smile. 'Your mum said you might be popping in, Archie. Looking to do some kind of project, she said.'

'Yes,' said Archie, thinking quickly. 'I'd like to make a new sweet for Unquiet Night. The McBudge factory doesn't make anything especially for the festival, does it?'

'No – it's an interesting notion, all right, Archie. But haven't you heard? Unquiet Night has been cancelled.'

'I only want to make a small amount of sweets. Just enough to … to test out something.'

Archie was going to take on the responsibility of being Guardian, but on his own terms. He was going to create something new. The Gingerbread Dragon was going to get an Archie McBudge *upgrade* …

21

The day of Unquiet Night arrived. It was blisteringly hot, and Dundoodle was smothered by a blanket of sticky air that caused sleepless nights, bad tempers and sweaty, bum-shaped patches on seats. All the windows of Honeystone Hall were open to let the air circulate, sending miniature dust storms and cobweb-paragliding spiders through the hundreds of forgotten, empty rooms.

Archie awoke, exhausted, from a feverish dream about Dragon-fire and jewels (and a badger called Clive) to find a red leaf lying on his bed. Written on its surface, in golden ink, were the words:

The Tree begins to shed its leaves. Tonight it must be renewed or all magic fails!

It was a depressingly unhelpful message from the Fjurge Brownies. A reminder of how desperate things were. He had failed to find the Treeheart. It was the very first time he had been called into action as Guardian, and he hadn't been up to the responsibility.

Archie checked his clock – it was almost afternoon! Why hadn't someone woken him? He'd gone to bed very late, after working with the others on his idea in the factory, but he hadn't meant to sleep in this long. He wasn't even sure his idea would work, either. Had the factory workers been able to make it successfully? He sprang out of bed and quickly got dressed, picking up Belle's journal from his bedside table. He'd kept it close ever since they'd found the secret writing on the recipe.

Running downstairs, he grabbed some toast from the kitchen and, followed by Sherbet, went straight to the factory. Billy and Fliss were already there, waiting for him anxiously in Mr Fairbairn's office.

'We'd thought you'd be here ages ago,' hissed Fliss. 'Archie, it's *Unquiet Night*. I hope you've got a Treeheart hidden under your T-shirt, or we're in trouble.'

'I haven't,' Archie growled. He was tired and scared, his temper frayed, but he still managed a smile when

Fliss's dad appeared, carrying a metal bowl of sweets. They were round and looked a little like marbles, with a swirling yellow and orange pattern.

'One experimental sample of our newest product,' said Mr Fairbairn, handing Archie the bowl. 'The very first sweet invented by young Mr McBudge. I have to say, I'm very impressed with your creativity and hard work. What did you say you were calling them?'

'Fizzfires,' said Archie. 'I hope they do Belle McBudge proud.'

Thanking a puzzled Mr Fairbairn for his help, Archie carried the bowl up to the hideout, followed by the others, panting in the heat of the factory. Blossom had been hiding in Fliss's bag and Fliss was eager to let the dragon out.

'It's already hot enough, without having to hide a dragon about your person,' she said, as the creature flew out of her bag and buzzed about the twisted pipework. 'Especially one that's all fidgety because she doesn't like sharing her transportation.'

'Sharing with who?' asked Billy, as Blossom let out a smoky grumble.

'Cogswallop,' said Fliss, showing Billy the clockwork dragon from Miss Clabbity's shop, which was sat at the bottom of her bag. 'That's what I named it. Blossom gets a bit jealous.'

'Completely bonkers,' muttered the real-life dragon, as she threw a withering look at the toy, from her perch on Sherbet's head.

'It's going to get hotter, I'm afraid,' said Archie. 'A quick blast of Dragon-fire on the sweets will finish them off. Then we'll have a replacement for the Gingerbread Dragon, something that will protect us from the Mirk – but with a twist.'

Blossom obliged, filling the metal bowl with golden flames. It wasn't enough to melt the sweets, but Archie could sense the magic in the air as the honeystone crystals formed. The Fizzfires were now enchanted.

'Belle's Gingerbread Dragons had honeystone in them,' said Fliss. 'I still don't get what makes these different.'

'They're smaller, but they have loads more ginger,' said Archie, 'so they're much more powerful. Belle didn't have a sweet factory nearby and that's our advantage. I added sherbet so they have plenty of fizz, just like our Sherbet! They're practically explosive!'

'It feels like you're handing out ammunition,' said Billy apprehensively.

'We're going into combat,' said Archie. 'We'll need every weapon we can get hold of. Magical sweets, dragons and battle-dogs included.'

Sherbet whined.

Archie divided the sweets between three small bags with long string handles and handed one each to Fliss and Billy.

'We'll take these with us on the boat to the forest,' he said, hanging the bag around his neck.

'I hate to be a bore,' said Fliss, 'but we're still missing one rather important jewel-related item. Without it, these sweets are pointless.'

'I know!' snapped Archie. 'Do you think I don't know? I'm just as frustrated – more so – than you! This is the best I can do right now.'

Fliss turned red and bit her lip.

Archie sighed. 'I'm sorry,' he said. 'I can't think straight in this heat – let's get back to the Hall, it's not so warm in there.'

The long, corridor-like portrait room allowed for the most movement of air, so the children went there to let tempers cool off. Archie slumped on the floor in front of the painting of Belle McBudge. Again, he reminded himself of the last part of the riddle from Belle's grave:

Look where my mournful gaze alights
One heart broken, one renewed.

'Billy,' he said, staring up at the portrait. 'Have you found any other pictures of Belle?'

'No. This is the only image that exists, as far as I know.'

'Do you think there's a clue to the Treeheart in the picture?' asked Fliss.

They stood up and studied the painting. Belle's gaze was a bit mournful, but what was she looking at? She was looking at herself in a mirror, and she wore a jewelled headband entwined with her hair.

'She's wearing jewels!' said Archie. 'Is one of them the Treeheart?'

'There's that scroll about the McBudge jewels, in the library,' said Billy running off to fetch it. 'And I can think of some other records that might help us.' He came back with a stack of parchment and several books, spreading them out on the floor.

Whilst Billy and Fliss divided the books between them, Archie opened Belle's journal, flicking through its pages, searching for any mention of jewellery. Perhaps she had written where she kept her headband – a hiding place for her treasured possessions? The old-fashioned handwriting was so difficult to understand!

Time passed. More books were found, more dusty old documents brought out, but none were of any use. Fliss even suggested a room-by-room search of the Hall.

'That would take *years*!' said Billy, pacing the room for the hundredth time. 'It's practically an expedition. We've only got a few hours left!'

'It's no good,' said Archie finally, sinking to the floor. 'We're doomed. Magic in Dundoodle is doomed.' He stared up at the painting. 'Come on, Belle,' he pleaded. 'Please help me. I really want to do this. *Please.*'

22

From nowhere, Archie caught the scent of spice: ginger. Was Tablet cooking? As the windows were open, the smell could have come from anywhere. But he remembered how the same scent had led them to Belle's portrait in the first place. He closed his eyes and inhaled. His mind began to clear, and he felt his senses sharpen. Opening his eyes again, he stood up in front of the picture, this time saying aloud: *'Look where my gaze alights.'*

Archie noticed something about the mirror Belle was looking at in the painting. She wasn't looking at herself. She was using it to look *behind* her, over her shoulder! She was looking at the little statue of Corignis, the dragon who died to save the Wyrdie Tree. The green eye of the dragon flickered. Archie frowned.

'Hang on,' he said. 'Honey dragons have golden eyes, not green!' And it was blinking at him! No, not blinking – it was glinting! There was a green jewel embedded into the picture itself, sunk into the wooden panel on to which the portrait had been painted. *This* was what Belle was gazing at! 'The Treeheart has been hidden in the painting all along, right under the noses of generations of McBudges.'

Archie lightly touched the jewel. The painted dragon suddenly moved its head and transformed. The whole picture was enchanted! Corignis was now a real dragon, clinging to the painting with very solid-looking claws.

As they watched in astonishment, the creature's eyelids opened wide, like a flower opening its petals. The left eye was the usual golden colour of honey dragons, but the right was emerald green and sparkling. The little dragon blinked and the jewel dropped out of its eye and into Archie's waiting hand.

'I've found it!' Archie laughed with relief. He could hardly believe it. 'The Jewel of Renewal. Clever old Belle. What a great hiding place!'

'I bet the wood that was used to make the painting came from the forest,' said Billy, 'from one of the magical trees.'

LADY ARCHIBELLE M^cBUDGE
(1478–1560)

The dragon – which now had two golden eyes – settled back into the picture and didn't move again. The Treeheart had been handed on, from one Guardian to another, and it was Archie's responsibility now.

Fliss and Billy gasped as the jewel sparkled in Archie's hand, spots of bright, green light reflecting on to the surrounding walls.

Fliss's bag began to rattle and jump about violently.

'Whoa!' said Billy. 'Have you something else alive in there?'

'No,' said Fliss, dropping the bag to the floor. 'Only Cogswallop.'

At that moment, the little clockwork creature waddled out of the bag, and began running in agitated circles at their feet. Then its wooden wings began to flap and the dragon took off, whirring in a spiral as it flew.

'I've never seen Cogswallop do that before,' said Fliss, with a laugh. But the hairs on Archie's neck stood up. There was bad magic at work here. Before he could act, Cogswallop swooped down, his jaws plucking the Treeheart from Archie's fingers. They watched, horrified, as the toy flew bumpily out of the room.

'Jewel thief!' yelled Billy. They raced downstairs after

the clockwork dragon, Sherbet running in front and barking angrily.

'I don't understand it!' said Fliss, stuffing Blossom unceremoniously back into her bag as they ran out of the open front door of the Hall. 'What does Cogswallop want with the Treeheart?'

'It's not Cogswallop,' said Archie. 'Preen must be controlling him.'

'But –' began Fliss. She was remembering something, but there was no time to talk. The thief swept down the drive, into the street and towards the factory gates, high over the heads and placards of the N.I.C.E. protestors, who were still outside and had grown in number, despite

the heat. Luckily, Mr Preen was nowhere to be seen. The children tried to make their way quietly through the crowd, hoping to go unnoticed.

'That's Archie McBudge!' said a voice that made Archie's heart sink. It was Miss McTwang, who was carrying a banner that said NO SUGAR – I'M SWEET ENOUGH, THANK YOU!.

'Please, let us through!' begged Archie. 'It's really important!' The protestors weren't prepared to listen. A large group had surrounded them, chanting. He recognised some of their faces.

'CHUCK OUT CHOCOLATE!' It was Mrs Crumple who ran the hillwalking club. She *always* had an emergency chocolate bar on her, in case she got stuck up a mountain!

'STAMP OUT SWEETS!' That was Old MacTwistie, whose usual hobby was sitting on street corners waving his walking stick at cyclists for no apparent reason.

'N.I.C.E. NOT NAUGHTY!' And that was Angus Beanfrost. He hadn't been near a dentist in years!

'MY BANNER IS ON FIRE!' shouted Peony Prestwick, which was a bit of an odd slogan. 'No, it really is – look!'

Whilst attention was on Archie, Fliss had opened her

bag, allowing Blossom to poke her head out for a moment and send a burst of flame upwards. One sign had caught alight, and others quickly followed. There were screams and shouts from some of the protesters as they tried to keep the burning card away from themselves, and people ran in every direction, throwing the placards to the ground and stamping on the fire to put it out.

Archie and the others took advantage of the confusion and hurried into the street. Through the smoky haze, they just caught sight of the clockwork dragon as it turned a corner.

'Where's he going?' said Billy, as they trailed after it. 'If we're not careful, we'll lose him in all this smoke.'

'It's not smoke,' said Archie, fear rising in his voice, as tendrils of fog crept around their feet. 'It's that Mirk mist – like we ran into in the old forest! And the dragon is heading for the graveyard …'

23

Archie was right – Cogswallop was fluttering towards the tower of St Bawgbreath's Church. They ran through the crooked lanes of Dundoodle, sweating in the late afternoon heat, as the mist thickened into a dank soup. The streets were empty, people either choosing to stay indoors to escape the weather, or wary of being out on this particularly eerie day.

'I don't like this,' said Billy. 'I don't like it at all. Going back to the graveyard when the Mirk is about. On Unquiet Night! It'll catch us, chew us up and spit us out like rancid liquorice! And that's if the restless dead don't reach up out of their graves and grab us first!'

They trailed the *click-clack* of the toy's wooden wings through the haze. It bobbed unsteadily over the wall of the graveyard. Following as quickly as they could, they just managed to see the dragon land, and scuttle through a small gap in the entrance to the McBudge vault. The green sparkle of the jewel was lost in the darkness inside.

'A dead end!' said Fliss, whispering for some reason.

'Literally,' said Billy with a nervous gulp. 'Those coffins are in there! We can't go back in.'

They stopped at the door. Sherbet sniffed the air, warily.

'We've got no choice,' said Archie. 'Without the Treeheart, the Wyrdie Tree can't renew itself. We're going in to face whatever's in there. Those coffins are only boxes of wood, remember.'

They cautiously heaved the door open, its metallic scraping sound all the more ominous in the mist. Fliss switched on her torch and the three carefully trod their way down the stone steps.

'Silent,' whispered Fliss, 'as the *grave*.' Annoyed, Billy gave her a nudge in the ribs. It was cold too. Facing them, in the middle of the tomb floor, was Cogswallop. He sat motionless, the Treeheart still held tightly between his clenched teeth.

'What's he waiting for?' said Archie. At that moment, there was an eerie cry from somewhere in the town: long, haunting and inhuman. It echoed amongst the tombs. It was a summons.

THUMP. THUMP. THUMP.

There was a dull clapping noise, a drumming from further down in the vault's deepest shadows.

THUMP. THUMP. THUMP.

It was getting closer.

'What is … that?' squeaked Billy, his throat dry.

THUMP. THUMP. THUMP.

Archie dragged the others back towards the steps, just as three hunched figures appeared out of the darkness. Scrawny arms and legs had sprouted like twisted tree-branches from squat, angular, headless bodies.

'The coffins!' squealed Fliss. 'They've come … alive!'

THUMP. THUMP. THUMP.

The coffin-creatures stepped jerkily towards them. The drumming sound was made by their lids slamming shut with each step. As the lids closed, the torchlight caught the children's names scratched on their surface.

'Coffin creepers!' said Billy. 'Like in one of the old Unquiet Night legends! Creepy Scale rating nine point seven! Though I might consider revising that, on the basis of first-hand experience.'

'They're after *us*!' yelled Archie. 'We need to get out of here NOW!'

'What about Cogswallop?' said Fliss, but Sherbet had already thought of that. The little dog pounced on the toy, grabbing its wings in his mouth. He ran up the steps and out of the door, and the children ran after him, as fast as they could.

THUMP. THUMP. THUMP.

The coffin creepers stomped after them.

'Where do we go?' said Billy urgently, as they scrambled out of the graveyard and into the town.

'The Hall!' said Archie. 'We need to get to the boat. It's the quickest way to the Tree.'

They charged through the maze of streets, leaving the creepers behind. But as they turned a corner they found their way blocked by a misshapen silhouette – one of the monsters had got there first! In horror, they retraced their steps, then took as snaking a route as they could, hoping to confuse their pursuers. But somehow the coffin creepers knew exactly which way to go, and always managed to block their path. The children were being herded, hunted relentlessly. The drumbeat of the coffin creepers' march was all around.

THUMP. THUMP. THUMP.

The fog was getting worse, it was difficult to see what was ahead. Dundoodle had sunk into an unnatural twilight, weighed down by the sticky heat.

'Miss Clabbity's is this way!' said Fliss, pointing down an alley. 'We can hide in there. Quick!'

THUMP.

THUMP.

THUMP.

The children stumbled along the cobbles;

fearful of every shadow, the heat pressing down on them, every footstep a superhuman effort. They saw the toyshop, its welcoming window lights dimmed by the mist.

'Thank goodness!' said Fliss, pushing open the door. 'We can barricade ourselves in with Miss Clabbity whilst we wait for rescue. She'll know what to do.'

'No,' said Archie. Something wasn't right. The feeling of dread – that he thought he was close to banishing with his newly found determination – was fighting to take over his head again. But Billy had already pushed him into the shop, and slammed the door behind them. Sherbet gave a throaty growl, still holding tightly on to Cogswallop. A figure stepped from the shadows inside. A smile gleamed menacingly.

'Do come in, children,' its owner said. 'I was expecting you, ha ha.'

It wasn't Miss Clabbity. It was Edward Preen.

'It's a trap!' squealed Billy. 'Caught between the Dentist of Darkness and the Triplets of Terror!'

'The creepers weren't chasing us!' said Archie. 'They were forcing us to come here.'

'Calm yourself,' said Preen, leaning towards the boy and grabbing his wrist tightly. 'Emotional agitation is hardly *nice* behaviour is it? But then you weren't keen on my Safer Wafer. Such a pity – it would have made things so much easier, ha ha.'

'The Safer Wafer,' nodded Archie. 'We worked it out. Anyone who eats a wafer is on your side.'

'Correct. The folk of this town need to be kept quiet this Unquiet Night. No music, no songs, no Dance of the Wyrd.'

'What's the Dance of the Wyrd got to do with anything?' said Archie.

'Quiet, boy! My work here is almost done. I need only to open the door and let in the coffin creepers.' The man advanced towards them. 'And that will be the end of you, ha ha.'

'You're not the only one with magical food,' said Archie fiercely, as they backed away. Sherbet dropped Cogswallop and barked protectively. The man gave a dismissive laugh.

'Gingerbread dragons? Unfortunate fool! I think you'll find there are none left in the entire town. My campaign has seen to it.'

'No, there aren't,' said Archie, reaching for the bag of Fizzfires at his neck, 'but we've got something *better*.' He scoffed one of the sweets and yelled to the others. 'Eat the Fizzfires! They'll protect you from Preen's magic!'

Billy took a sweet from his bag and stuffed it into his mouth. 'Hmmm, they're tasty …' he said, eagerly chewing the Fizzfire. Then his eyes went wide. 'And fizzy – my mouth is tingling like I've a mouthful of glow-worms!

And you weren't wrong about the extra ginger. They're super-fiery! That's quite an upgrade on the gingerbread.'

For the first time, Edward Preen was not smiling. He glowered at them.

'Yes – that's something else you don't like,' said Archie. 'Fire. I saw you at the twins' party, when Portia inciner-ated your cake – goodness knows how many people you were planning to bewitch with that – you were hiding from the fire! And we've got our own source!'

Fliss knew immediately what she had to do and pulled at the bag which contained Blossom. 'I can't open it,' she said desperately. 'Blossom – are you all right?'

Preen swung around, his eyes filled with malice, just as a blast of flames scorched a hole through the bag from the inside and the little dragon's indignant face poked out. The man cried out as Blossom wriggled free and soared in circles around the shop, firing bursts of embers and smoke. Preen sank to the floor, shielding his head with his arms. Then he lay very still. Too still.

'Is he … dead?' said Billy. 'Because if he is, I know where he can get a coffin for free.'

'The coffins!' said Fliss suddenly, as the little dragon landed on her shoulder and stroked her cheek with its nose. 'I remember everything! Oh, Archie! Miss Clabbity …'

Archie was crouched over the unmoving dentist. There was something odd about him. He still had his smooth features – his dark hair, his smile and his cold eyes – but he was … changed. His face looked more chiselled, more polished …

'He looks like he's made of wood,' says Archie. 'He looks like –'

'Archie,' said Fliss. 'Listen to me! Miss Clabbity –'

'A puppet,' said Miss Clabbity, appearing from the back of the shop, through a door they hadn't noticed. 'He looks like a puppet. Because that is what he is – carved from wood and magically brought to life.'

'So that's why he was afraid of fire!' said Billy.

'How do you know all this, Miss Clabbity?' said Archie.

'How do I know?' said the old lady, smiling. 'Fliss knows. She was trying to tell you. I know because *I* made him, of course ...'

'You made him,' repeated Archie, turning very pale. His head was suddenly rocked with pain. 'You're behind all this – *you're* the Mirk!'

Miss Clabbity kept smiling, but it wasn't a nice smile. It wasn't a human smile.

'I've waited five hundred years for tonight. Five hundred years, to fully regain my power. Hiding inside this shop, using my puppets, human or wooden, to do my bidding.'

'But you can't be the Mirk!' said Fliss, close to tears. 'Miss Clabbity's a nice old lady. She makes toys. I've seen her outside the shop, everyone has!'

'That was the real Miss Clabbity,' the monster said, its eyes turning pure white. It walked to the display of puppets and picked up Red Riding Hood's grandmother, who Archie had noticed looked so much like the old toymaker. 'And here she is. I turned her into one of her own toys when I assumed her identity. I wanted her to know what it felt like, after she carved the last bit of Mirkthorn, my *home*, into one of her playthings.'

Miss Clabbity's voice had turned into a growl, and her teeth were now pointed and glistening. She dropped the grandmother and picked up the Mirkthorn puppet, eyeing its spiky, black surface with affection.

'She found the last surviving piece of Mirkthorn wood in the forest, all that was left after the dragons thought they had destroyed it. Something told her what shape to carve – a wicked plant that binds and strangles.' She laughed. The laugh was dark and cruel. 'Little did she know.'

Miss Clabbity began to grow, her shadow filling the shop. Her back arched and her woolly old-lady clothes merged into a twisted monstrous body. It was as black as the night, covered in needle-sharp spines which moved unnervingly. Archie screwed up his eyes and could see the creature's hide was covered in jet-coloured earwigs, woodlice, centipedes and spiders, their constant silent wriggling making the spines writhe as if they were alive. They dripped on to the floor like boiling oil. Her hands twisted into claws and her smile transformed into a hungry, drooling snarl. Then she raised her head and let out a cry that, despite the heat, turned their blood to ice. It was a cry of triumph.

The children huddled together in a corner, as the monster that had been Miss Clabbity towered over them, glaring at them with its white eyes, its spines bristling. Archie clutched Sherbet to his chest, whilst Blossom seethed quietly from Fliss's shoulder, holding the Mirk with her golden-eyed stare.

'Why would you do all this?' said Archie, his fear momentarily giving way to anger. 'With Preen, and the N.I.C.E. campaign? Was it just to get rid of the Gingerbread Dragons?'

'I feed on the dark magic that is set free every Unquiet Night, and my strength grows,' said the Mirk. As it stepped forward, black fungus and toadstools grew where its claws trod. 'But only after five hundred years do I have enough to take my true form and act. Preen was my instrument, whilst I was not fully powered. Crafted from enchanted trees that I cut from the forest, he had a useful sorcery of his own that I could manipulate. And the bark became the magic ingredient in his wafers. As well as removing the cursed biscuits, he distracted and dispirited you, weakening your resolve. I am a creature of darkness and decay. I rot people's souls, corrode their fortitude and consume their happiness. Just like I did with your ancestor.'

'But Belle McBudge beat you!'

'At what cost? Her beloved dragon burned itself out defending her. It broke her heart!'

'You really are not very nice *at all*,' said Billy, with some understatement. Archie was raging.

'But you failed in the end!' he said. 'You thought you'd stop her from protecting the Tree, but she did it! And she made the Gingerbread Dragons, as a memento and a warning to the future. It worked, and it's not too late. We have the Treeheart and we're going to the Wyrdie Tree, right now.'

He went to grab Cogswallop but the Mirk pointed a bony claw at the toy and it came to life once more, flying to the monster's feet. The Mirk extracted the jewel from

its jaws, then cast the toy aside, where it smashed to pieces against the wall.

'Now that I have the Treeheart,' the Mirk said, throwing the jewel on to its back, where it was caught amongst the spines, 'the Wyrdie Tree is powerless against me. The Dance of the Wyrd shall not take place.'

From all corners of the shop, hundreds of little wooden toys rolled forward – soldiers, trucks and animals, gathering around the evil spirit. They carried saws and axes, ropes and hammers, their clockwork whirring and clicking as they moved. It was the insect-like sound that Archie remembered from their encounter with the Mirk in the forest!

'My army of helpers,' explained the Mirk. 'Useful for cutting down trees, particularly very *large* trees, so I can get to their roots. And you cannot stop me. You may be protected from my magic by your sweets, but I have ways of keeping you *busy*.' It unleashed another horrible cry.

THUMP. THUMP. THUMP.

'Uh-oh,' said Billy, looking out on to the foggy street. Three lumpy outlines were crowded around the shop window. 'The coffin creepers are here, and they look like they mean business.'

'We *will* stop you!' called Archie, as the snarling monster turned and squeezed its massive bulk out of the shop door, attended by the clockwork army. 'There has to be a way.'

'We'd better think of it soon,' said Billy. 'As we're about to be boxed up like a batch of McBudge Fudge – a human-flavoured special edition.'

THUMP. THUMP. THUMP.

The coffin creepers plodded up the steps to the door, ducking clumsily to enter the shop. The children and dog backed away, desperately looking around for a means of escape. Fliss had a grim look on her face. Then she stopped suddenly.

'That's it!' she announced. 'I've had enough. I've been bewitched, made to argue with my friends, tricked into helping a jewel thief and chased around town by some fancy wooden crates. It's time to kick some magical-tree butt! Let's see what these guys can do with a bit of fire, Blossom!'

The little dragon soared up to the ceiling. Dragon-fire was unleashed on the first of the creepers, singeing the rough wood of its body, and sending curls of smoke into the air. But the monster kept on coming.

'Try a Fizzfire, Blossom,' said Archie, throwing the creature a sweet from his bag. 'It might give you a boost.' Blossom caught the sweet mid-air and gulped it down, before sending a second burst of fire at

the smouldering coffin-man. This time the flames were an electric blue, exploding with a power they had not seen coming from a honey dragon before. The creeper was engulfed in the magical inferno, collapsing to its spindly knees, before falling to the ground with a final *THUMP*.

'That's *my* coffin taken care of,' said Fliss, folding her arms and looking at the boys. 'What are *you* going to do about yours?'

THUMP. THUMP.

The remaining coffin creepers stepped over the smouldering body of their fallen comrade, closing in on the children. Blossom readied another burst of flame just as Sherbet let out a bark of warning. Archie thought it was aimed at the monsters but the dog was looking beyond them, to a figure in the doorway. A blade of bright silver ripped through air towards them and sliced across the front of both coffin creepers, scoring through the names carved on the lids. Instantly, their arms and legs shrivelled away to nothing, and the coffins dropped to the floor with a harmless clatter. The blade boomeranged back to the figure, who caught it with an arrogance Archie recognised.

'It seems I've arrived just in time,' said the figure. It was Mrs Puddingham-Pye.

26

Despite the heat, she was dressed in a long black coat that swirled about her like the fog that was creeping into the room. In one hand, she held the silver knife. In the other, a skinny broom. Garstigan sat on her shoulder, leering at the fallen coffin creepers. He was still wearing the yellow doll-hair, Archie noticed.

'If that's your Unquiet Night costume, it's very authentic,' said Billy. 'Eight out of ten on the Macabre Creepy Scale.'

'I prefer the traditional look, at times like this,' said Mrs Puddingham-Pye, with a smile that was almost warm. 'I just saved your lives, by the way.'

'Thank you,' Archie said, and he meant it. He'd

been more scared than he realised. 'How did you know we'd be here?'

'I sensed the Taciturnitas Hex had been lifted,' she said, tucking the knife into her belt. 'Presumably when Preen was ... deactivated.' She cast a glance at the wooden ex-dentist, crumpled on the floor.

'Then Garstigan spied the boxy men in the street,' hissed the mobgoblin, fussily plumping his ringlets. 'Told his mistress, and we followed their clumpy foot-steps. So noisy!'

'The coffin creepers are wood golems,' his keeper finished. 'They're enchanted by a simple spell and easy to neutralise. All you need to do to is strike through the name on the lid and they don't know who to chase.'

'Or you can use your own personal magical flamethrower,' said Fliss, smugly patting Blossom's head.

'A tactic of which my own dear daughter would approve.'

'Does this mean you're *helping* us?' said Archie.

'As I said before, Urchin, we've a common enemy. I've no wish to see the end of magic in Dundoodle any more than you. So, yes, we have a temporary truce. But if you were in possession of your wyrdworking powers, you wouldn't need my help.'

'What do you mean?'

'For example, just like Preen, these coffin creatures were made from timber taken from trees of the old forest, enchanted trees. The same enchantment is at the root of your powers. Your powers come from the forest itself – you could easily have commanded the golems to stop, if you'd known how.'

'That would have saved us a *lot* of trouble,' said Billy.

'I don't have time for lessons, right now,' said Archie. 'Or any more talking. We need to get to the Wyrdie Tree. The Mirk is on its way to destroy it. And I may not be able to wyrdwork, but I've got to do something!'

'I said the coffins were yours to command,' Mrs Puddingham-Pye impatiently. 'Make use of them, boy!'

'We've already got a boat to get us across the loch,' said Billy.

'I don't mean anything so dull.' The woman marched over to one of the coffins, and stepped into it. She rapped the handle end of her broom on to the floor of the wooden box. Blue lightning rippled down the broom and the coffin rose off the ground, hovering steadily.

'You, Bilbo!' barked Mrs Puddingham-Pye, pointing at Billy. 'Get in!'

He was too stunned to argue. He scrambled inside the coffin and sat down, nervously.

'Now, boy,' said the woman, looking at Archie. 'It's your turn. The coffin is your servant. Command it, make it do your bidding. Order it to fly.'

Archie felt confused. He didn't like the idea of commanding anything. He wasn't like Mrs Puddingham-Pye. Her way wasn't *his* way.

'Do it now, boy!' the woman snapped. 'There isn't any time to lose!'

Archie stepped into the other coffin. He touched its chiselled sides gently, remembering how the tree stumps had felt when they had found them in the old forest, the painful sense of destruction he'd experienced. It was time for this wood to return to the place where it had grown from a seed, and lived for so many years, before it was cut and cruelly manipulated by the Mirk. He felt the coffin's surface grow warm. A breeze blew through the town, sweeping in through the door, and the fog retreated. The air suddenly began to cool, and as it did the smell of fir trees, birch and oaks, bracken, heather and cool streams swirled around him – the same scent of the forest which he had smelled the day he met the Wyrdie Tree. He felt its strength flow through him.

'Let's go,' he said softly. The coffin wobbled, then lifted shakily off the floor.

'You're doing it!' squealed Fliss, 'Archie, you're doing it!' She jumped into the coffin and sat down. Sherbet dived in after her and sat himself in her lap.

'Good, boy!' snarled Mrs Puddingham-Pye. 'Think of the destination – focus on it in your mind.'

The coffins sailed out of the shop and climbed above the alleyway, Billy and Fliss hanging on to their sides for dear life. The fog was now being scoured from the town, as cooler air swept across the loch and pushed the unpleasant heat away. It was as if nature were joining them in the battle against the Mirk. Archie had to concentrate to keep the coffin airborne in the breeze, and not tip them out over the rooftops, but after a couple of wobbly moments he began to feel more confident. Mrs Puddingham-Pye stood regally as the wind rippled around her, her black coat flying out behind like a raven's tail.

'Onward, boy!' she yelled across to Archie. 'Onward!'

'If she had a whip,' muttered Fliss, 'she would be cracking it. I reckon you've got the hang of your magical powers.'

'I think they've got the hang of me,' said Archie. 'It's like they're a pair of shoes that have put themselves on my feet and after a few days of hobbling around, finally they're starting to fit.'

The strange flying-craft sped out over the loch. The low sun poured orange light across it, turning the water the colour of fire.

'We need to go to Pookiecrag Island,' Archie called. 'Jings said the honey dragons would help us!'

Mrs Puddingham-Pye nodded, and the coffins steered towards the ruins of the castle. As they approached, gliding over the tumbledown turrets, they could see something was wrong.

'What's that plant growing everywhere?' said Billy, leaning dangerously over the top of the coffin, making it

wobble so much that Mrs Puddingham-Pye had to poke him with her broomstick. 'It wasn't there before. And I have to say it's more Creeping Beauty than Sleeping Beauty.'

The whole castle was covered in a black, prickly vine that had wrapped itself tightly around the stonework.

'Is it Mirkthorn?' said Archie, jumping out of the coffin as it landed in the centre of the ruins. 'Careful of these spikes, they look deadly!'

'It's not a plant,' said Billy. 'It's metal. A net of barbed wire.'

The web-like net appeared to spread out from a single point: the fireplace that hid the tunnel to the Cavern of Honeystone. Blossom flew to the fireplace and vainly tried to burn the metal away.

'This isn't just the Mirk's handiwork,' said Fliss miserably. 'It had help.' She pointed to a black wooden star that was fixed to the trapdoor in the hearth. The web had grown from its points, spreading outwards over the castle, and sealing the trapdoor with its stranglehold. There was no way to get the door open – the dragons were trapped!

'That's the toy Miss Clabbity gave you,' said Archie. 'The puzzle. You said you'd lost it.'

'I *had*,' said Fliss. 'Or at least, I thought I had, but I must have left it here on purpose, after we visited the dragons. It wasn't a toy at all, it was another bit of nasty magic! When Miss Clabbity said the lady and the dragon were her favourite puppets, she was talking about me and Cogswallop! We were her puppets. Archie, what have I done?' Fliss sank to her knees. She looked distraught. Blossom landed softly on her shoulder and licked her cheek.

'You've always supported me,' said Archie gently. 'Always pushed me along to do the right thing, made me see sense. You know this isn't your fault. Preen, the Mirk – they were controlling you.'

'But this is like what happened to Belle. She faced the Mirk with just one dragon, and look what happened! I don't want to lose Blossom!'

'You won't! There's a team of us here and no one is going to die.' Archie pulled her to her feet. 'Don't be sad, Fliss. Don't be scared – be angry! Proper, Felicity Fairbairn angry!'

She looked at him and grinned.

'You're completely bonkers, Archie McBudge,' she said. Then a cry echoed from across the water.

'We're wasting time!' snapped Mrs Puddingham-Pye. The children climbed back into the coffins and they rose once more into the air, speeding towards the old forest.

There was no mistaking the Wyrdie Tree itself. Towering over everything else, with its bright red foliage, it stood out like a beacon ablaze. But there were bare patches visible up and down its length, as leaves fell and were cast about in the breeze. The moment of Renewal was approaching.

They raced over the treetops towards it, spiralling around the Tree's vast crown as they carefully descended on to the circle of grass beneath, now carpeted with crimson leaves. The leaves were falling faster, revealing more of the Tree underneath. There were little windows in parts of its aged and cracked trunk, perhaps the home of the brownies or other magical folk. The brownies themselves were waiting on the ground, their eyes fearful. They had been in this situation before, hundreds of years earlier.

'The Mirk is upon us!' cried Dubbeljøk, as Archie jumped out of the coffin. The squirrel sat on the brownie's head, squeaking in agitation. 'Its cries get ever closer. It's destroying everything in its path! Do you have the Treeheart?'

'I ... did,' said Archie. 'The Mirk stole it from us. But we'll get it back, I promise.'

The brownies clasped their hands together and looked at each other in despair.

'We're doomed!' said Jøkchip. 'The Tree will be infested with darkness! All magic shall be controlled by the Mirk. And we shall be devoured by the monster.'

'Cheer up!' said Billy, popping a Fizzfire into his mouth. 'It's not over yet – try one of these. And we brought reinforcements.'

The brownies viewed Mrs Puddingham-Pye and Garstigan with distrust.

'You shall rue the day you made a pact with this dark-hearted harridan and her sky-rat,' grumbled Jøknut. Mrs Puddingham-Pye rolled her eyes and Garstigan glared at the man's robin like it was a potential snack.

'Magical types are always so overdramatic,' Mrs Puddingham-Pye yawned. 'And less of the "harridan", if you

please, mud-pixie. You need all the help you can get, like it or lump it, and you'll need it very soon or you'll all be garden ornaments.'

The Mirk's choking fog was seeping into the clearing and coiling around the stone circle. Then, with a noise of sawing and grinding, a cluster of trees suddenly crashed to the forest floor at the circle's edge, their leaves shrivelling and dropping to the ground as their trunks ruptured and turned black. The Mirk was rotting everything it touched.

Billy and Fliss – with Sherbet and Blossom – took up position on either side of Archie on the leaf-strewn slope, whilst Mrs Puddingham-Pye whispered to Garstigan behind them. The Fjurge Brownies kept close to the Tree, protective of their charge, as its last leaves rained down around

them. Under a cloud of gloom, the Mirk's monstrous form slunk out of the forest, surrounded by its clockwork army.

'The Tree is mine,' it growled, its voice full of hunger. It held the Treeheart up in a spiny claw, laughing at its victory. 'You cannot stop me.'

'I am still the Guardian and I *will* stop you,' called Archie defiantly. His mind was churning with anger, and fear. He needed to concentrate but it was too hard: he hadn't a clue what he was doing. Why did *he* have to be the Guardian? Why couldn't someone smart like Fliss do it? Or someone knowledgeable, like Billy? He wasn't up to the job. Doubt seeped in. The dread began to overwhelm him again.

Archie felt a stab of warmth at his chest, coming from his bag of Fizzfire. There was a scent of ginger in the air, just like when he had stood by Belle's portrait. Maybe Belle was still looking out for him. Again, he felt his senses sharpen. His dread left him.

It's a trick of the Mirk, he thought, *sapping my confidence and making me question myself, just like Preen bewitched everybody*. He ate a Fizzfire and felt its warmth flowing through him.

He silently called to the forest to help him. The leaves at his feet leaped into the air and flew at the approaching monster. Like a flock of birds, they raced around the Mirk, enclosing it in a tornado of red and gold, urged on by Archie's willpower. The Mirk sneered, piercing the column of leaves with its claw and turning them to dust. But the distraction was working.

'Blossom,' Archie said. 'Let's give the toys a little heat.'

He threw the dragon another Fizzfire, which it happily gulped down. With a deep breath, Blossom sent an explosion of blue flame straight at the wooden toys, which were crawling like ants at the Mirk's feet. The fire swamped them and they burned brightly, trapping the monster in a circle of flame. It snarled angrily.

'You won't stop me!' it roared. Fingers of fog reached forward to dampen the bonfire of toys.

'What can we do?' yelled Billy, over the noise. Fliss grabbed a handful of Fizzfires from her bag.

'Maybe these can help keep the fire going,' she said. She hurled the sweets into the flames. They instantly exploded with an orange crackle and the fire burst back to life, stronger than before. Billy threw another handful of sweets, and the flames rose higher and brighter.

'The Fizzfires really are weapons!' he said with delight.

Archie glanced back at Mrs Puddingham-Pye.

'How are we going to get the Treeheart?' he said. 'We

can't hold the Mirk off forever.' The woman's eyes glittered.

'All is in hand, boy,' she said. Archie noticed Garstigan had disappeared from her shoulder. He looked overhead and saw the bat-like creature silhouetted against the sky. It swooped over the wall of fire, as fast as a hawk, ripping the jewel from the distracted Mirk's claw. The monster roared in fury, but Garstigan was gone, his ringlets slightly singed, back to his mistress's outstretched hand. He dropped the green stone into her palm.

'Pretty shiny thing for the mistress!' he said.

Mrs Puddingham-Pye's eyes coldly studied the Treeheart.

'At last,' she said. 'I was beginning to think it would never
happen. The power of the Wyrdie
Tree is now in *my* grasp.'

There was a sharp intake of breath from the brownies.

'We told you not to trust her!' said Dubbeljøk.

'You can't be serious!' said Archie, staring at the woman in disbelief.

'Why not?' Mrs Puddingham-Pye clutched the jewel tightly. '*I* should be the Guardian of the Wyrdie Tree, not you. *I* should have access to all its power. I could use the jewel to strip the Tree if its magic and bind it to me. Think of what I could do!'

'We are,' muttered Billy. 'But whatever you do decide to do, do it quick – the Mirk isn't going to wait around for you.'

The monster had almost quenched the blaze, despite the combined efforts of Archie, Billy and Fliss's Fizzfires, and the supportive barks of Sherbet. It clambered through the smoke and fog, over the ashes of its army, and angrily lumbered towards the tree.

'I'm the Guardian, and I can't change that,' said Archie to Mrs Puddingham-Pye, thinking fast. 'You could take the jewel for yourself, take all the magic, but then what? Eventually the magic will run out. You don't have access to its source, deep in the earth, like the Tree does. The Mirk will come for you and what will save you then? I won't be able to help. We *must* work together. There's no way either of us can destroy the Mirk alone – we need each other, you said that yourself, or else there'll be no magic for anyone. Please – give me the Treeheart. I'm the Guardian and it's my job to do this.'

Mrs Puddingham-Pye was silent for a few agonising milliseconds. Then she tossed the jewel in Archie's direction.

'I wasn't *really* serious,' she said, with a casual sigh, though Archie had caught her shiver at the idea of the Mirk coming after her, 'but it was amusing to wonder at what might have been.'

Archie ran – the Treeheart in one hand, Fizzfires in the other – up the slope to the Wyrdie Tree. Its branches were now completely bare, with the exception of one lonely red leaf. Any second now, that leaf would fall and the Tree would be a skeleton of itself, vulnerable, unable to renew until the Treeheart was in place. The Mirk knew this as well.

It was the monster's last chance. With a horrible growl, the Mirk charged at Archie, trying to cut him off before he could reach the Tree. Archie was almost there, but the monster was easily gaining on him. It leaped at the boy, its black, bony claws stretching out to seize him. A bolt of blue lightning shot from Mrs Puddingham-Pye's broom and knocked the Mirk out of the air, sending it crashing into the earth with a terrible howl, just as the last leaf gently floated to the ground.

For a moment, there was silence. The Tree stood starkly against the sky. It did look sad and defenceless for something so huge. Archie knew he had to protect it. He took a deep breath and slammed the jewel into the notch in the bark.

'I've done it,' he gasped with relief.

The Tree shuddered, as a green light spread from the jewel through the cracks in its bark, like blood through veins. As it flowed up the Tree and streamed around its many branches, buds appeared, which instantly burst into leaf. On and on the light went, further up to the topmost boughs. Soon, the Wyrdie Tree was covered once more in a vibrant, vital green that shone in the evening sun.

Archie could feel the Tree's magic growing with it. All his fears and doubts disappeared – it was as if he were recharging along with the Tree. The Mirk hissed and spat angrily, looking at Archie with a boiling hatred.

'You may have beaten me,' it growled, 'but I'm not finished! I will return in another five hundred years, then again and again until the end of all things!'

It planted a claw on the ground, sending black toad-stools and fungus crawling towards Archie, killing all the grass as it surged forward. Mrs Puddingham-Pye fired her broom at the Mirk, but whilst it held the monster back, it wasn't enough to stop it.

A thought appeared from nowhere in Archie's mind. *Fight darkness and decay with light and life.* Was the Tree

talking to him? Or another voice – was it Belle McBudge, giving him one last piece of help? He raised his hand, pointing at the Mirk. A tree root erupted from the earth in front of him, driving through the fungus and wrapping itself around the Mirk like a snake, squeezing and holding it tight.

'He's properly wyrdworking!' said Billy delightedly.

'Archie!' said Fliss. 'Are you making that happen?'

'Me and the Tree and Belle McBudge!' said Archie, frowning in concentration.

'You heard what the boy said earlier,' called Jøkchip to Mrs Puddingham-Pye, who stood watching Archie with surprise. 'It'll take both of you to destroy it.' She nodded and sent lightning from her broom into the Mirk's body. Then Blossom joined in, breathing flames at the monster, as Billy and Fliss hurled more Fizzfires at it. The Mirk writhed and howled under the united attack, and began to shrink before their eyes.

'It's working!' shouted Billy. 'Go on, Archie!'

The root coiled tighter and tighter, trying to crush the darkness. The Mirk fought back but shrank more and more, its body gradually weakening and fading.

'I may fade,' it shrieked at them, 'but you cannot destroy me! Not whilst the last piece of Mirkthorn remains.'

'Oh, yes we can,' said Fliss. Calmly reaching into her tatty, fire-scorched bag she pulled out a toy – a black, thorn-covered puppet. She dangled it in front of the Mirk, the monster's face distorted in horror. 'I brought this with us from the shop. Thank you for reminding me.'

Blossom unleashed her furious fire on the puppet, instantly turning it to a cinder.

'That was for Belle,' said Fliss, treading the puppet's ashes into the earth. 'And for Corignis.'

With a final, desperate cry, the Mirk shrivelled to nothing. Without a host for its spirit, it was gone forever.

Archie dropped to his knees in exhaustion, and wiped the sweat from his brow.

'You did it!' said Fliss, running up to him and giving him a hug.

'*We* did it,' said Archie.

Billy kicked at the black fungus.

'Thank goodness that's over,' he said. 'I never want to eat another mushroom again.'

29

The Fjurge Brownies gently picked Archie off the ground. Their faces were beaming with joy.

'The Wyrdie Tree is saved,' said Jøknut. 'And the Mirk utterly destroyed. The forest's wounds will heal and all will be green once more. This is an Unquiet Night to be remembered!'

'You have proved you are worthy to be Guardian,' Dubbeljøk added. 'We're sorry we ever doubted you.'

'And you've learned to wyrdwork,' said Jøkchip. 'We can help train you to be better at it. But you used reason and the common good to convince others to help you.' He looked at Mrs Puddingham-Pye, who was picking up a Fizzfire from a number that had dropped from Archie's bag. 'The Mirk had to use magic to get others to do its bidding – your humanity, your care for others, is one power that it could never understand.'

'I also had friends,' said Archie, grinning at Billy and Fliss. Blossom snorted a contented cloud of smoke, whilst Sherbet almost wagged his tail off with happiness.

'This is a *delightful* scene,' said Mrs Puddingham-Pye, sauntering up to Archie. 'But I must be on my way – my job here is finished.'

'Thank you for helping us,' said Archie. 'Maybe we don't have to be enemies, after all.'

Mrs Puddingham-Pye gave him a hard stare for a moment. Then, taking the Fizzfire she had picked up, she crushed it in front of his face and let its dust trickle to the ground.

'You are unbearably, sickeningly good-hearted, Urchin,' she said. 'We will *always* be enemies, you fool. The truce is *over*.'

She threw the broom into the air and jumped expertly on to it as it began to soar into the sky.

'Come, Garstigan,' she commanded. The mobgoblin grumbled to himself, then grabbed some Fizzfires and stuffed them in his greedy mouth before following his keeper. As they flew over the treetops and out of sight, Garstigan burped a little blue flame that caught, unnoticed, on the end of the broom.

'The broom could burn up just when she's flying over the loch,' observed Billy. 'If we're lucky.'

More lights appeared in the early evening sky, moving rapidly. Blossom gave a burst of happy fire and soared up into the air to meet them.

'The honey dragons!' said Fliss. 'They're free!'

A swarm of the little creatures, including Old Jings, landed gracefully on the grass. The brownies bowed low in greeting. The elderly dragon explained that the net trapping them in the cavern had disintegrated into black dust and blown away on the breeze.

'We knew immediately you must have vanquished the Mirk, and flew straight here!' said Old Jings. 'The McBudges would be proud of you, young Guardian. Belle can rest in peace.'

'And Corignis,' said Archie. He told them how the Treeheart had been hidden in the statue in the painting. 'He played his part in defeating the Mirk, too.'

'Now we must get you home,' said Old Jings. 'Before the Dance of the Wyrd takes place.'

'I want to see it!' complained Billy. 'And I don't want to get in that coffin again.'

'The wyrdie-folk are shy,' said Jøknut, 'and won't be needing you humans present at their festivities. Perhaps the dragons and my brothers can provide an alternative means of transport.'

The Fjurge Brownies ran back to the Wyrdie Tree and produced a large blanket from a nook in its trunk that, like their cloaks, was made from hundreds of woven leaves. The children and Sherbet stepped on to the surprisingly soft cloth as the dragons picked up its edges, lifting it off the grass like a magic carpet.

'We can use the coffins to grow vegetables in,' said Dubbeljøk, scratching his beard thoughtfully, as Archie and the others were carried away over the loch. 'As long as they don't get up and run off with my turnips.'

The journey back to Dundoodle was much more relaxed. Archie realised how hungry he was. He'd barely eaten all day. Billy was quiet, remembering all the wyrdiness he had witnessed, so he could write about the experiences later. Fliss had dozed off in the blanket's warmth, exhausted by everything they had been through.

Archie looked down on the town of Dundoodle below, its lights starting to appear, a mirror to the stars emerging above them. The dragons' scales sparkled as they flew, reflecting the fire-bursts from their mouths, and surrounding the children in a warm light.

There were still questions that needed answering.

'What is the Dance of the Wyrd?' Archie asked Old Jings. 'The Mirk didn't want it to happen. Preen said he wanted the town to be quiet, with no music or singing.'

'On Unquiet Night, the dark magic of the universe is let out to play and the Unpeople make mischief,' said the dragon. 'But they cannot be allowed out for long or there would be chaos. The Dance is the ceremony the good wyrdie-folk perform that locks it back in the earth for another year. If there was no Dance then the dark magic would be freed for good, food for the insatiable appetite of the Mirk. And the Dance needs music.'

'Music,' said Archie, 'from Dundoodle's festival?'

'It is a link that binds humans to the Wyrd. They have to play their part in the magic, just like you do as a Guardian. That's why the Mirk wanted it stopped.'

'But the festival *was* stopped!' said Billy 'What will happen to the Dance, without music?'

The old dragon smiled to himself.

'We'll see,' he said.

The dragons left the children in the garden of Honeystone Hall, before buzzing off into the night. Blossom flew away with them, to spend some time with her relatives, after her encounter with the Mirk. She'd seen some things that would scare even a dragon!

Mum saw them walking up the drive.

'There you are!' she said, opening the front door. She seemed a little flustered. 'I've been looking for you for ages.'

'We've been for a … walk,' said Archie innocently. 'There wasn't much else to do, seeing as the festival was cancelled.'

'That's just where you're wrong!' said Mum with a smile. 'Unquiet Night is back on. I've just been called by the organising committee! I don't quite understand what's happened, but that dreadful Mr Preen vanished with the fog, then there were fireworks overhead, and suddenly everyone is in the mood for a festival again. What's up with these people? There must something in the water.'

The children looked at each other as sounds of music floated up from the town. They left Sherbet safely with Tablet then, with Mum following behind, hurried down the street to Dundoodle's market square. It was already filled with people, stalls and tables, all lit up by lanterns hung from the surrounding buildings. People were bringing out heaps of food: Witchberry buns, toffee apples and Wyrdie-pudding, Spooky Pie, Corpse Rolls and Coffin Cakes.

'I think I'll give *those* a miss,' said Billy, eyeing the Coffin Cakes. 'It's a shame there are no Gingerbread Dragons. Preen got rid of them all.'

'It doesn't matter,' smiled Archie. 'They're not needed. And I'm sure they'll be back next year.'

They had a go at 'Bite the head off a Water Sprite', which Fliss won, and 'Guess how many skulls in the pile o' skulls', which Fliss also won, and a three-legged race called 'The march of the Triskelion', which Fliss also won (with Mum), much to Billy's annoyance.

'I should be studying paranormal activity, anyway,' he said huffily. 'Not playing silly games.'

Then there was the puppet show. To Fliss's delight, the real Miss Clabbity appeared in a little theatre tent with her puppets, none the worse for her time spent as one of her own creations. The Mirk's spell had broken, leaving her with no memory of what had happened. She was puzzled as to why there was a burned coffin in her shop, but Dundoodle *was* an odd town. The lady and the dragon appeared on the stage of her theatre, to cheers from the crowd, but no Mirkthorn appeared that night, or ever again.

There was a costume parade, with children in their best (and worst) home-made outfits, ready to go on the Wyrdie Walk and bag as many sweets as possible, without Mr Preen to interfere.

Then there were proper fireworks. They were no match for the honey dragons, but they still lit up the sky

with a rain of stars and sparkling fountains of bright colour. The crowds clapped and squealed and laughed, and – clinking glasses of Spellcaster Sugarbeer together – agreed they were much better than last year's.

Finally, someone brought out some bagpipes, and violins and drums and tin whistles appeared too, and the music began. Everyone joined hands, forming a chain of people that danced through the streets, weaving in and out of the alleyways and the lanes. Archie was surrounded on all sides by happy, dancing people and could feel the magic of Unquiet Night in the song and the movement and the joy. It tumbled into the air, away over the loch, and if he had been able to, he would have seen another dance taking place beneath the Wyrdie Tree, a circle of strange folk dancing together,

to the same tune as the people of Dundoodle, lit by the fire of a flight of dragons.

Archie was stood in the portrait room of Honeystone Hall. Was he imagining it, or did the painting of Archibelle McBudge look happier than before? He had picked some heather from the dragons' moor and placed it on her tomb a few days after Unquiet Night, as a way of saying thank you. It felt like the right thing to do, a proper end to her chapter in the story.

None of the townsfolk of Dundoodle ever knew what had become of Mr Preen. As far as they were concerned he had just disappeared, and with him had disappeared their appetite for all things N.I.C.E. They discovered they were actually quite fond of sweets, after all.

The McBudge factory would be producing Fizzfires for the next Unquiet Night. Mr Fairbairn said they were already proving very popular with test groups, and that Archie's future as a sweet-maker looked very bright indeed. Almost as bright as Billy's future as a historian. He was made an honorary member of the Dundoodle Historical Society, in recognition of his discovery of Belle McBudge's original recipe for Gingerbread Dragons – the youngest ever person to receive the award.

Fliss wasn't fully her normal self for a while. Her confidence had taken a knock. She did not like being used and was horrified that she could have worked against her friends. She was too stubborn for the mood to last, however, and she was soon back to arguing with Billy, or teasing Archie, and her bond with Blossom was stronger than ever.

'I thought I might find you here,' said the ghost, who appeared through the wall of the portrait room, at Archie's side.

'Great-Uncle Archibald!' said Archie. 'I thought I was never going to see you again.'

'I wanted to properly congratulate you on your good work, Archie. You've already achieved more than most Guardians do in a lifetime. I can see you are going to have an eventful future.'

Archie grinned.

'I'm ready for it,' he said. 'There was a while when I thought I wasn't. But I know now that being the Guardian is what I was meant to do. And I'm happy to do it, as well. I belong here.'

The ghost smiled.

'I'm glad to hear it.'

'It was you who helped us find the map to the Wyrdie Tree, wasn't it?' said Archie. 'The atlas flying off the shelf and that sudden breeze were your doing.'

'Aye, it was me,' Great-Uncle Archibald admitted. 'I thought you could do with a hand. Since Belle's time, all the McBudges have used her map to get to the Wyrdie Tree. I was shown it by my father, so I thought it was fair enough to provide a bit of spiritual guidance. I don't think you need my help any more.'

'I hope I do,' said Archie. 'I think I would miss you, if you were gone for good.'

'I meant to ask you,' said the ghost, its misty eyes getting mistier for a moment. 'What did you do with the Treeheart after the Wyrdie Tree had renewed? It has to be kept safe for the future. Where did you hide it?'

The boy gave the ghost a sly smile. Sunlight shone through the elderly phantom, beckoning Archie outside.

'It's quite safe,' he said, whistling for Sherbet and running for the door. 'Where? You'll only have to wait five hundred years to find out …'

Acknowledgements

I would like to award the Freedom of the Town of Dundoodle to the team at Bloomsbury Children's Books for all their hard work in making *The Dentist of Darkness* a thing of actual paper and ink. Their patience, enthusiasm and eye for detail has made the experience a total pleasure. I'd also like to usher onto the podium all the book bloggers, reviewers and influencers who had such nice things to say about *The Chocolate Factory Ghost*, giving The Dundoodle Mysteries such a great start in life. I hope this book is enjoyed just as much!

An extra-large medal goes to Claire Powell for her fabulous illustrations and to the children at the Tom Fletcher Book Club launch who helped her create the fearsome Wood Waggle.

Read about Archie's first adventure!

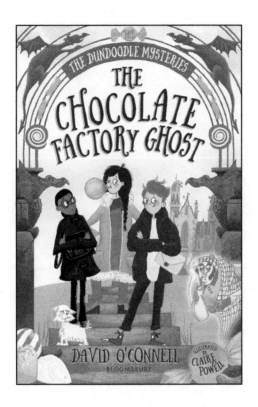

AVAILABLE NOW

Turn the page for a sneak peek!

1

Archie stared up at the portrait of the old man. It had winked at him, hadn't it? He was sure of it. No, he must be imagining things. This spooky old house was playing tricks with his mind.

He was sitting in the very grand library of the very grand Honeystone Hall, surrounded by books – how could anyone own so *many* books? – and ancient, rickety and *very* dusty furniture. Were all the cobwebs real or were they specially delivered by the We'll-Make-Your-Home-Look-Creepy Company? Mum sat in the chair next to him, fidgeting like she had spiders dancing in her underwear and too preoccupied to pay any attention to misbehaving artwork. Had the portrait winked at him again? It hadn't. Had it? It HAD! It even grinned a little. This place was seriously WEIRD.

He dragged his eyes away from the painting which hung above the very grand fireplace.

'What are we *doing* here?' he whispered for the hundredth time.

'I don't *know*,' Mum whispered back. She gave the sparrow-like man shuffling papers, who sat in front of them, a sharp look.

'Can we get on with … *things*, Mr Tatters?' she said. 'We've come all the way from Invertinkle.'

'Of course, of course, dear lady,' said the lawyer amiably. 'Some of the details of this … *situation* are unusual. I was just checking a few particulars, but now we can proceed.' He cleared his throat dramatically.

'Archie McBudge,' said Mr Tatters, peering at the boy through a pair of grubby spectacles. 'You are a very fortunate young man. Very fortunate *indeed*. Great things lie in store for you.'

Archie had never thought he was destined for Great Things. A few Medium-Sized Things perhaps. 'Medium-sized' always sounded manageable. Great Things sounded like a *lot* of responsibility and he wasn't the ambitious type.

'Really?' was all he could say. *What was going on?*

'Whilst we mourn the recent *tragic* loss of your

great-uncle, Archibald McBudge ...' said Mr Tatters, pointing a bony finger towards the painting – *the* painting! He had a *Great-Uncle Archibald?* '... owner of McBudge's Fudge and Confectionery Company, and a dear, personal friend of mine ...' Archie's jaw dropped. McBudge's Fudge! He'd never even known Great-Uncle Archibald existed, but everyone knew McBudge's Fudge. It was the softest, sweetest-tasting, melt-in-the-mouthiest, fudgiest fudge you could buy. The best in the world. Archie had always been pleased he shared his name with a company that made something so famously tasty, but he'd never thought there might be an actual family connection! And from the look on Mum's face, she hadn't either. She started to say something but was interrupted by Mr Tatters giving his beaky nose a good blow.

'Whilst we mourn his loss,' the lawyer repeated, dabbing his eyes, 'I am very pleased to tell you that your great-uncle remembered you in his will.' He picked up a leather-bound folder. Archie and Mum looked nervously at each other. Nobody had ever left them anything in a will before. They'd never known anyone with any money! All they knew was that Mr Tatters had sent them a letter asking them to drive all the way to the little town of Dundoodle, tucked between a mountain and a forest-edged loch, to meet him at Honeystone Hall to talk about some 'family business'. The lawyer was reading from a piece of paper in the folder.

'Your great-uncle writes: *As my nephew is no longer alive, I hereby leave all my earthly possessions to his son, my namesake, Archie McBudge. My fortune, my business holdings and associated properties I leave to him and his heirs.*' Mr Tatters took off his spectacles and looked at Archie expectantly.

'Oh, Archie!' said Mum with a deep intake of breath.

'What?' said Archie. He didn't understand. What were 'earthly possessions'? 'Has he left me his gardening tools or something?'

'No!' hissed Mum. 'Archie, he's left you *everything.*'

'Everything?' said Archie.

'*Everything,*' said Mr Tatters.

'Does that mean I *own* the fudge factory?' said Archie in disbelief. 'Where they make the fudge and the chocolates and all the other sweets?'

'Yes, Archie. You own the fudge factory,' confirmed Mr Tatters.

'And all the McBudge Fudge shops?' put in Mum, wide-eyed. 'There's one in almost every town.'

'And all the McBudge Fudge shops,' said Mr Tatters.

'And Honeystone Hall?' said Archie, looking around him. 'Can we come and live here? There must be over a hundred rooms in this place!' And a very odd painting, though he didn't mention that.

'*And* Honeystone Hall,' said Mr Tatters. He snapped the folder shut. 'Fudge fortune. Fudge factory. Fudge shops. Fudge … urm, *Honey*stone Hall. The whole lot. Even the gardening tools.'

I must have put my lucky underpants on today, thought Archie. He looked up at the portrait of Great-Uncle Archibald. The old man in the painting winked at him again. And this time, Archie winked back.

2

'There's one more thing,' said Mr Tatters, reaching into his jacket pocket. 'Your great-uncle left you this letter.' He handed Archie a crumpled envelope. A surprisingly steady hand (Great-Uncle Archibald looked *ancient* in the portrait) had written on it in thick caramel-brown ink:

To the heir of the Chief of the Clan McBudge.

'The heir,' said Mr Tatters, catching Archie's puzzled look. 'That would be you. Old Mr McBudge intended for you to read this in private. Why don't you go and explore whilst your mother and I discuss the legal paperwork and whatnot? I'm sure you'll find plenty of quiet spots in the house to read.'

He was being dismissed. The grown-ups had grown-up things to talk about. With a nod from Mum, Archie ran out of the library, clutching the mysterious letter. His head was spinning. He was … he was *rich*! And Honeystone Hall belonged to *him*. Him and nobody else. Except maybe the ghost of his great-uncle. What had been going on with that painting? He pushed it out of his mind. There were plenty of other things to think about. Great Things. It would take him a week just to explore the house, never mind the gardens and the factory.

Archie wandered along a passageway, pondering which of the doors to try first. Everything – furniture, pictures, wallpaper – looked *very* old and was covered in a ghostly layer of dust. The stillness was deathly. *Plenty of quiet spots*, Mr Tatters had said. Spots? This was practically measles.

He tried one door. It was a cupboard, filled with moth-speckled coats. Another door revealed an old-fashioned laundry room, with sinks and mangles and drying rails. So far, so disappointing. Yet there was something else. In each room Archie could feel a presence, like someone – some*thing* – had left just moments before. He shivered.

Finally, he chose a large green door with a dark metal handle. With a satisfying clunk, it opened and light poured into the shadowy passage. He took a step backwards as he was struck by the heat and smell of earth. Ferns, palm trees, vines and orchids lay before him, bathed in a balmy mist and occupied with the business of growing and flowering and generally being alive and leafy. Had he stumbled into a different world? Transported to a desert island? He half expected a dinosaur to lumber into view.

'It's a giant greenhouse,' he said aloud. The glass roof was as high as the Hall itself. The warmth, light and life were a marked contrast to the rest of the house and the dreary wintry world outside it. But it had the same watchfulness about it. Something hidden had its eye on him.

Archie followed a path amongst the plants and perched on a twisted tree root that had pushed its way up through the tiled floor. He opened the envelope and pulled out a crisp piece of paper covered with the same caramel-coloured writing.

Dear Archie (the letter began),

Mr Tatters must have told you by now that you are my heir as Chief of the Clan McBudge, as well as heir to the McBudge Fudge fortune. I have no doubt this will have come as a surprise to you. Knowing you would inherit one

day, but wanting you to have a normal life for as long as possible, your father kept his family connections a secret.

So Dad knew all along! Archie smiled. Dad loved secrets. He wished Dad was here now.

Your father was a clever man. Having lots of money can do strange things to people. And the desire for money can make people go bad. Very bad. You must always remember this!

But who better to run a chocolate factory than a child? Children understand fudge and sweets and chocolate far better than grown-ups. However, it is a great responsibility.

You must prove you are worthy of your inheritance, worthy of the name McBudge! So I have set you a test, in the form of a treasure hunt, to see just how canny you are ...

There are six items you must collect, and six clues to find them. Once you have them all, a greater seventh treasure awaits you! But keep it secret! Others will go to any length to get it first!

Others? What did that mean?

The first clue will appear very soon. Keep your eyes open and your taste buds ready! You may find help in the strangest ways. Dundoodle is an odd place – expect the unexpected ...

Good luck!
Your great-uncle, Archibald McBudge.

Archie realised he was holding his breath. His heart was beating fast. A test? A treasure hunt?

P.S. Look behind you.

'If you ask me,' said a voice just by his ear, 'you're in a whole lot of trouble, Archie McBudge.'

ARCHIE, FLISS, BILLY and SHERBET
will be back in the next book in

THE DUNDOODLE MYSTERIES

COMING 2020